Serenade/Serenata · 17    AN INSPIRATIONAL ROMANCE · $2.50

# The Desires of Your He[art]

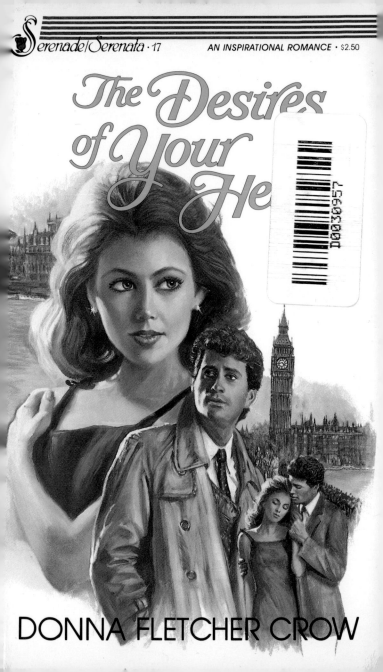

# DONNA FLETCHER CROW

**"Sandy, I just wish I could tell you how happy I am . . .'**

wrote Pam. "It's so beautiful sharing our spiritual relationship as well as the physical. The oneness Brad and I feel while praying together is as wonderful as the oneness we feel during the most intimate moments of our marriage.

"I'm convinced that a truly Christian marriage is the closest relationship on earth. After all, the closer two objects are to a central point, the closer they are to each other."

The letter continued, but Sandy couldn't concentrate. She now saw with absolute certainty how right Pam and Brad were for each other. Both the revelation and the relief were startling. Though she had once imagined herself in love with Brad, she now knew how wrong their marriage would have been. The release was like a fresh sea breeze blowing through her mind. "Thank You, thank You, thank You," she said over and over again, and then laughed aloud.

She grabbed her pen and stationery to tell Pam how truly happy she was for her. But after the first line, the words wouldn't come and her pen hung poised in midair. She thought of Martin Graham—and the strange fascination he held for her—and the words of Pam's letter swam before her eyes: *sharing our spiritual relationship as well as the physical . . . a truly Christian marriage is the closest relationship on earth . . ."* That was what Sandy desired with all her heart—but she could never have that complete unity with Martin.

*How could you?* she berated herself. *How could you possibly fall in love with a man who doesn't share your faith?*

# THE DESIRES
# OF YOUR
# HEART

*Donna Fletcher Crow*

𝒮*erenade*/*Serenata*
**BOOKS**

**of the Zondervan Publishing House
Grand Rapids, Michigan**

## A NOTE FROM THE AUTHOR:

*I love to hear from my readers! You may correspond with me by writing:*

Donna Fletcher Crow
1415 Lake Drive, S.E.
Grand Rapids, MI 49506

THE DESIRES OF YOUR HEART
Copyright © 1985 by Donna Fletcher Crow

Serenade/Serenata is an imprint of
The Zondervan Publishing House
1415 Lake Drive, S.E.
Grand Rapids, MI 49506

ISBN 0-310-46702-0

*Edited by Nancye Willis and Anne Severance*
*Designed by Kim Koning*

Scripture quotations in this book are excerpted from *The New English Bible*. Copyright © The Delegates of the Oxford University Press and the Syndics of the Cambridge University Press, 1961, 1970. Reprinted by permission.

*Printed in the United States of America*

85  86  87  88  89  90  /  10  9  8  7  6  5  4  3  2  1

*For Sandra*
*my proper English friend*

# CHAPTER 1

SANDY HOLLIS LOOKED out at the gray clouds drizzling rain and the sea of black umbrellas sailing by on the wet tarmac of Heathrow Airport. *London*. Her throat tightened with excitement and her eyes misted like the window of the plane. She wanted to sit and just *look* until her mind could absorb the fact that she was here.

But the "Fasten seat belt" sign had blinked off and everyone, anxious to deplane after the eight-hour flight from Boston, was scrabbling for personal belongings.

Sandy reached for her purse on the empty seat beside her, a sharp wrench at her heart threatening to squelch her excitement. Ironic that one of the few empty seats on the flight should have been next to hers. The seat shouldn't have been empty at all. For the briefest moment Sandy

7

allowed herself to imagine what sharing this experience with Brad would have been like. Then she staunchly shut the door on the thought and groped under the seat in front of her for her flight bag and the umbrella she had been advised to keep at hand.

She waited for a break in the line of passengers filling the narrow aisle before stepping into the opening.

"Ouch!" she cried as she fell back unexpectedly against the seat. A strong masculine arm in a camel's hair blazer pushed out in front of her, catching her off balance.

She looked up at him in amazement, gasping at such rudeness, and rubbed her thigh where she had fallen on the arm of the seat. He had his back to her and was fully engrossed in escorting a petite woman with enormous dark eyes into the space he had cleared for her. He ushered the woman forward with a protective hand on her arm, and she gave him back an intimate smile.

Sandy opened her mouth to protest, but the couple moved down the aisle, seemingly lost in each other.

Close behind them bustled an enormous woman in a bright blue coat, carrying two overstuffed shopping bags. Fuming, Sandy fell in behind her, amazed that the woman could negotiate the narrow passage.

After the hassle of baggage claim, customs, and passport inspection, Sandy emerged into the fresh, wet air with relief. Umbrellas, seemingly propelled by their own power, hurried past, and cars sprayed water onto the already puddled sidewalk.

Juggling two worn suitcases, her flight bag, and purse, while attempting to shelter herself under her umbrella was no easy task, but Sandy's real attention was focused on hailing a taxi. Each time she spotted an unoccupied vehicle, someone less burdened and therefore quicker than she grabbed it first.

"There, finally!" she muttered aloud, seeing her chance, and shouting, "Taxi!" she rushed toward the quaint high-roofed black cab. Only a few feet from the door, her grip on the damp suitcase handle slipped and the piece of luggage crashed to the sidewalk. Fortunately the lock held, but she lost the taxi—to the fat woman in the blue coat. Frustration spurred Sandy's determination. A second taxi pulled into view and, sloshing through an ankle-deep puddle and waving her umbrella in desperation, she started forward.

With an almost exact replay of the exit from the airplane, the camel's hair blazer suddenly appeared in front of her. This time, however, she was not barricaded by just an arm, but by a broad back. The abrupt movement in front of her caused Sandy once again to lose her grip on the suitcase handle.

Twice was too much for the old case and with

a sickening snap, the lock sprang open, disgorging the contents onto the wet pavement. While Sandy was scrambling around, rescuing her belongings, and getting thoroughly soaked in the process, the little sloe-eyed coquette was escorted, dry and comfortable, into Sandy's taxi.

*Enough is enough!* Angrily, Sandy stepped right off the curb into the running gutter and boldly stood her ground until the next taxi could not fail to stop for her.

By the time she reached her hotel, the rain was letting up and the sky was beginning to clear. Although still seething over her inhospitable treatment in the airport, Sandy's spirits began lifting with the clouds. After all, this was London—she couldn't let a little rain and rudeness dampen her enthusiasm.

Taking time only to hang her clothes in the closet and change her wet shoes, she went out again to get acquainted with the area around her hotel and to find a tea shop for lunch. With her heart singing, she walked down the uncrowded street now aglow under a watery sun. Here she was—Sandy Hollis, New England school teacher, vacationing for an entire summer in one of the most exciting cities in the world—living proof that dreams could come true, no matter how many had ended in disaster before.

Sandy looked around her, delighted with the people populating her dream: Two English school boys in their short pants, knee socks, and caps, chasing a wet, hairy little dog; a little old lady in a green cardigan sweater, with a scarf over her head and an empty shopping bag over her arm, apparently on her way to do the marketing; a middle-aged blond woman wearing a tweed suit and sensible, sturdy shoes. . . .

Sandy approached the woman. "Excuse me. I wonder if you could tell me if there's a nice tea shop nearby?"

"Oh, you're an American, are you?" asked the woman in her English accent, which was so pleasing to Sandy's ears.

"Yes, just arrived, I'm afraid."

"Well, let me show you, my dear. There's a lovely little shop only two blocks down this street." She started off, apparently expecting Sandy to follow.

"Oh, but I don't want to take you out of your way. I'm sure if you'll just give me the directions. . . ." Sandy hurried to catch up with her guide.

"No bother at all. I'm more than happy to show you."

"Thank you so much." Sandy was flabbergasted at the woman's kindness, and added, "Won't you let me buy you a cup of tea?"

"Oh, goodness no. But thank you just the same. You have a happy holiday now."

The shop was small and plain, but each table was set with a gleaming white tablecloth and linen napkins, and brightened by a fresh daisy in

11

a small vase. The tea was brought steaming hot—properly brewed, of course—in a round brown pot, accompanied with sugar, a jug of milk, marmalade, and a rack of crisp toast from which the crusts had been cut.

Sandy smiled as she poured the rich amber liquid into her china cup and added milk and sugar. In college, she had worked for the president's wife, helping with the many hostessing responsibilities of her position. Just one of the lessons she had learned was the proper art of pouring tea.

Sipping from her cup and admiring the simple elegance of the shop, Sandy was engulfed by the sense of graciousness and lack of hurry. She took a deep breath and leaned back in her chair, glancing at the only other occupied table in the little shop.

In the corner to her left sat a couple, only slightly younger than she. They had been served sandwiches and tea, but hadn't touched them. So totally engrossed in each other were they that Sandy doubted they had even noticed their refreshments. Sandy sighed at the empty chair at her table and poured herself another cup of tea.

As she sipped she allowed her thoughts to return to that night just two months earlier when Pam, her roommate, had wakened her from a sound sleep to announce her engagement—to Brad. Brad—the only man in whom Sandy had ever felt more than a passing interest, the only man with whom Sandy had ever thought she could build a life.

Before Pam captivated Brad with her golden blond hair and sparkling personality, Sandy and Brad had daydreamed of one day visiting England together. . . . *No!* Sandy admonished herself, spreading marmalade on a slice of thin toast. *You're not going to rehash that episode. You cared deeply for Brad, but Pam and Brad fell in love and that is that. Besides, Pam's your friend—you were even her bridesmaid.*

But the fact remained that the good things always seemed to happen to others. Sandy didn't begrudge their happiness—she just wanted her share. *Happiness,* she thought mockingly, remembering her tenth birthday when her whole family—both parents and a baby brother—had been killed in that terrible automobile crash. They had been on their way to Grandma and Grandpa's for her birthday party. It was a miracle she hadn't been killed, too, but she had been thrown free of the car before it burst into flames. Fourteen years had passed, but she still had nightmares.

Aunt Martha in North Platte had done her best to provide a home. She supplied food, clothing, and shelter; and with a discipline that stopped just short of harshness, had taught Sandy manners and the fear of God. And when Aunt Martha was no longer there to see to things herself, the provisions of her will sent Sandy to college.

13

But nothing or no one had been able to break through the emptiness Sandy carried inside her. No one until Brad . . . Sandy bit viciously into her toast, furious with herself for allowing such unhappy thoughts to accompany her to London. She was starting a whole new summer, a whole new life. In her brave new world, the possibilities were limitless.

Early that evening Sandy prepared for her first night in London. She had given in to fatigue and slept most of the afternoon. Now, feeling bright and rested, she surveyed her travel wardrobe: a well-coordinated ensemble of three suits with a variety of blouses and matching slacks and two dresses. She smiled to herself, recalling how long it had taken her to assemble those items.

On her limited salary from Meadowbrook Christian Academy, Sandy had become an expert bargain shopper—delighting in the high-quality clothes she could sometimes find at ridiculously low prices in Filene's basement in Boston, just a short bus ride from her apartment in Lexington. She had haunted the shop every Saturday for months for this special wardrobe. And being the first new clothes her budget had allowed for ages made them even more special. Tonight she would wear her beige suit with a coral blouse—might as well celebrate her first evening in London with her best foot forward, and this was probably the most expensive outfit she had ever owned, even though it had cost her only a fraction of its original price.

She laid out the suit, then hurried down the hall to the bath. Maddeningly, there was no plug, and the hot and cold water came out of separate faucets. She had to choose whether to be scalded or frozen.

But even if there had been no running water at all, she would have been excited about her plans for the evening. She did the best she could to survey her appearance in the dim mirror and dimmer light provided in her room. Her anticipation made her skin glow with even more than its normal luminescence and her dark blue eyes sparkled brightly. She brushed her shoulder-length curly brown hair until it fell around her cheeks, its amber highlights glowing in the light from her small lamp.

In studying the travel brochures, an open-air performance of Shakespeare in Hyde Park had been a must. Shakespeare on her first night in London—and free, besides! As if in honor of her arrival, tonight the players were doing one of her favorites, *The Tempest*. Perhaps she felt a certain kinship with Miranda—both had been raised in isolation.

She allowed herself plenty of time, and with her course charted carefully on her visitor's map, she walked the distance down Oxford Street to Hyde Park. The dreary rain of the morning had given no promise of the lovely evening. The setting sun tinged the clouds with gold and silver, as the evening air carried the scent of flowers from the boxes that adorned almost every window of the neat row of narrow brick houses with white front steps. The sound of traffic on the street and the pleasant English voices floating by her on the sidewalk were a symphony to Sandy's ears, and when a red double-decker bus lumbered by, she knew that the scene was complete.

Finding Hyde Park was simple enough, but locating the amphitheater was quite another matter. One could hardly follow the crowd, as there were clusters of people everywhere, none of them seeming bent toward a common goal. Finally Sandy gathered her courage and approached a young couple just ahead of her on the broad sidewalk. The girl's short blond hair curled charmingly over her forehead; the boy was taller by a head, his thick brown hair partially obscured by a tweed cap. Both were wearing tan raincoats and both had what Sandy could only describe as that wholesome English look.

Seeing their close, almost intimate, companionship, brought to Sandy's mind an unwelcome vision of Pam and Brad honeymooning beneath swaying palm trees in Bermuda. But she staunchly dismissed the scene and approached the couple. "I wonder if you could tell me how to find the Shakespearean theater?"

They turned with broad smiles. "Oh, of

course—that's where we're going! It's just up ahead." The girl pointed. "Come along with us."

Sandy was reluctant to intrude on their date, but they insisted she join them.

"I'm Karen Graham," the girl introduced herself, flashing her bright smile again.

"Bill Caxton," said her companion as Sandy offered her hand.

"You're American?" Karen asked.

"Does it really stick out all over?" Sandy laughed.

"Well, yes, it's hard to define, but you dress in a different way and you have a sort of confidence, and then, of course—your accent. Oh, but it's very nice," Karen added hurriedly, as if hoping she hadn't offended their visitor. "I most likely picked up on it more quickly because my mother's an American—from Baltimore. As a matter of fact, I was in your country just this spring, visiting my American relatives. I had a wonderful time—everyone was so warm and friendly."

Sandy was charmed with her new acquaintances and smiled in reply as Karen recounted her experiences in America. "I expect you've been there," Karen said about virtually every place her Auntie Elaine had taken her. But Sandy had never been to Baltimore or Philadelphia or Washington, D.C.—she had been busy saving every penny so she could go to London.

The theater was a large grassy dell bordered by

17

trees. The area sloped gently toward a stage constructed of stone and so completely surrounded by bushes that it looked as if it, too, had grown there. Sandy couldn't decide whether the small cave at the rear of the stage was a natural phenomenon or if it had been constructed just for the performance.

"Oh, but you haven't a rug," Bill said as they moved to an open spot on the grass.

"No, I didn't know." Sandy was dismayed— her beautiful new suit—and sitting all evening on the grass.

"No problem. You can share ours," Bill spread the plaid wool blanket on the ground, still slightly damp from the morning rain.

"But, your date. . . ."

"Nonsense! Sit," Karen said. "I don't get many opportunities to repay all the kindnesses shown me in America."

Sandy sat gratefully.

The dell filled quickly with people of all ages: Young couples, families with children, groups of elderly ladies—some even had their dogs with them. A few of the older people had brought colorful folding chairs and sat around the outside edges; their hues and those of the flower beds blended in a warm kaleidoscope of color in Sandy's delighted vision.

A butterfly flew past, adding to the enchantment, and Sandy knew that, finally, her turn for happiness had come. So many writers had described trips to England as experiencing a sense of homecoming, but Sandy, who for years had known only a foster home, dorm rooms, and rented apartments, had not expected to feel such an immediate sense of belonging. Especially since any actual family ties with Britain would date back three or four generations—maybe more. But there it was— deep joy and fulfillment and completion.

*Thank you, Lord*, she breathed silently. *I didn't expect this feeling outside of heaven*.

Suddenly the lights from the stage dimmed and a familiar melody filled the air. The audience rose to its feet and Sandy stood too, a soft "Oh," escaping her lips.

Karen smiled at her, "Do you know it, too?"

Sandy just grinned, feeling rather foolish. Of course the orchestra was playing "God Save the Queen." She had first thought it was, "My Country 'Tis of Thee." No matter how satisfied she may feel here, she still had some acclimating to do.

From the moment the lightning flashed and the thunder crashed and the actors rocked back and forth in their boat, tossed by the magical tempest on the stage, Sandy was held enthralled. Miranda was a beautiful young girl with flowers entwined in her long black hair, and Sandy felt her own heart swell with vicarious affection for Ferdinand as the young lovers discovered their "brave new world that hath such beauteous creatures in it."

And when Prospero declared in his rich, round tones that: "Our revels now are ended: These actors, as I foretold you, were all spirits and are melted into air, into thin air. . . . We are such stuff as dreams are made of, and our little life is rounded with a sleep," Sandy thought she would burst with joy and sadness at the same time.

And then it was over and Bill was folding the blanket and everyone was walking and talking and Sandy reluctantly pulled herself away from the enchanted island to the present. . . .

"I'm sorry, Karen. What were you saying?"

"I said, you'll come to supper with us now. We have a favorite place we want to show you. A tourist would never find it."

Sandy knew by now it was useless to protest, and besides, she suddenly realized that she had eaten nothing since her lunch of tea and toast.

"I'd love to!"

It was true that Sandy would never have found the place on her own. And, as Bill ushered them down a dark alley, illuminated by a single street light, she began to wonder if she wanted to. Finally, they descended a long flight of stairs.

"Are you sure about this place?" she asked.

Karen laughed. "You'll love it once you're inside! It's just the getting there that's questionable."

"This place is called the Underground," Bill said, pushing the door open for the girls.

"I can see why," Sandy responded.

But her friends were right. Inside, was a delightful retreat. The dark paneling and open-beamed low ceiling gave a feeling of intimate coziness and the fire blazing on the hearth of the rustic brick fireplace at the end of the room gave welcome warmth. There were a number of bare, dark-wood tables on the wide-planked floor, and candles and soft amber lights cast a mellow glow. Several other diners were already seated, but the room wasn't crowded. Bill led the way to a large round table near the fireplace.

"The table in the corner is 'our table'," Karen pointed. "But my brother is meeting us here tonight, too, so this will be more roomy."

Before Sandy had a chance to reply, the waiter, clad in black slacks and T-shirt with a white butcher's apron, brought a plate of steaming hot sausage rolls and a large pot of tea to their table. The pungent aroma of the spicy sausage bursting with juice and flavor inside its flaky puff pastry made Sandy's mouth water. She had no idea she was so ravenous.

"Specialty of the house. What you Americans call 'Appetizers,'" Bill explained. "We can order later if we wish. Here—they're best while they're hot."

Sandy needed no urging. She was almost through her roll when Karen let out a cry of delight. "Here he is!" She jumped from her chair to run to a tall man who had just entered the room. Sandy was still licking the sausage off her fingers when they approached the table.

"Sandy, this is my brother Martin Graham. . . ."

Sandy looked up. Karen was chattering animatedly about their new friend from America, but Sandy was too dumfounded to catch all the words. She had never seen the face before, but there was no mistaking the camel-hair blazer or those broad shoulders.

# CHAPTER 2

RESISTING THE URGE TO GAPE, Sandy registered the fact that Karen was standing with her arm around her brother, looking up adoringly at him. How could a charming girl like Karen have such a boorish brother? Sandy acknowledged the introduction coolly.

Martin held Karen's chair for her, then took the empty seat next to Sandy.

"Oh, Martin, you were gone for just ages. I want to hear all about it!" Karen offered the plate of sausage rolls to her brother.

"Nothing very exciting to tell—just dull business," he shrugged. "Lots of paperwork and boring chaps carrying briefcases. Airports are very much the same the world over." He obviously did not want to pursue the subject.

*And beautiful women with eyes like huge black*

*sapphires, and rude men pushing you about,*
Sandy would have loved to add. It was really
very amusing. The irony of the situation tickled
Sandy's sense of humor. Of all the planes flying
into Heathrow that day. . . . Of all the passengers
she could have bumped into. . . . Of all the
theatergoers who could have befriended her. . . .

"And how long have you been in London?"
Martin turned his deep brown eyes on Sandy.
She caught her breath. He was so tall and, with
his tendency to shove his coat in her face, she
had never seen how strikingly handsome he was.
He had that wonderful lean, bony look that one
always associated with Cambridge men: The
same long face with high cheekbones, the slow
smile, the square dimpled chin.

"Mmm, well, I guess it's about fifteen hours
now," Sandy smiled slowly, toying with the
situation.

"Well, welcome to London! Is this your first
trip?"

"Yes. I flew over this morning from Boston."
She wondered if he would put that together.

"Really? What airline?"

"British Air."

"Amazing! Do you realize we must have been
on the same flight?"

Her smiled broadened, "Yes, I do. As a matter
of fact, you got off the plane just ahead of me."

"No! Isn't that something?" He seemed at a

24

loss for words, but covered it by taking a sip of tea.

Sandy was surprised by his sudden display of nervousness. Everything she had seen of him had led her to believe he was as self-assured as a bulldozer and about as thoughtful. He glanced from her to Karen, then engaged Bill in a discussion. Something about a car. Sandy began to wonder if she had observed something she wasn't supposed to have seen, or that his sister wasn't supposed to know about—that woman, perhaps. Sandy glanced at his left hand. No ring, so apparently she wasn't his wife. Sandy smiled. He probably had a mistress and didn't want to shock his sister, who obviously idolized him. Karen was sitting now, her chin resting on her locked fingers, glowing with admiration for her brother who frequently turned from his conversation with Bill to smile at her.

Well, Karen was a darling girl, and Sandy wouldn't disillusion her. If she had a brute for a brother, that was her problem. But in spite of Sandy's absolute aversion to his manner, she was captivated by his strong features and the thick brown hair that lay across his forehead.

"And how long will you be honoring our sceptered isle with your presence?" Martin turned back to Sandy, the car talk finished.

"I have the whole beautiful summer," she replied with a sigh. "School doesn't begin until the first week in September."

"School?"

"Yes, I'm a teacher—English literature and drama—so of course, your sceptered isle is Mecca to me."

"What's first on your agenda?"

"Well, the usual tourist sights, the Tower, changing of the guard, Westminster Abbey, that sort of thing. But my real pilgrimage will be to Winchester."

"Winchester?" They looked at her blankly. "Why Winchester?"

"Jane's buried there."

They still didn't respond.

"Oh, come now—Jane Austen. Surely, English curriculum can't have slipped that far."

"Oh, yes!"

"Of course!"

They recovered rapidly. "Winchester isn't high on the national register of tourist traps, that's all," explained Karen.

"It's a beautiful drive there, but you've come a long way just to see a grave." Martin sounded bored with the idea.

*A bored boor*, Sandy thought and she had to suppress a giggle. "Well, that's hardly all. There's Bath and Glastonbury, and Cambridge, and—"

"Cambridge. Now there's a spot of luck," Bill broke in. "I happen to be a student at Trinity. When can you come up? I'll show you around."

Karen spoke before Sandy could answer, "I'm

going up next weekend. Why don't you go with me?"

"Intrude on another of your dates?" Sandy demurred.

Karen laughed, "Well, since we've been engaged for almost two years now, it isn't as if we needed to be alone to get acquainted—much as we do enjoy being together," she added, her warm smile resting on Bill. As he returned it, Sandy felt a familiar wrench at her heart. Would she ever be able to share that special understanding with someone?

"Are classes still in session? Or are you doing summer school?" she asked Bill, who was waiting for a response to Karen's invitation.

"Three more weeks—long vacation doesn't start until the end of June. Do come, we've planned a boating picnic and it should be quite jolly."

"It sounds irresistible—I'd love it."

The week flew by. Sandy spent one whole morning milling around Buckingham Palace, or "Buck House" as the British irreverently called it, then to Trafalgar Square with the other tourists and the flocks of pigeons. She joined the queue at the Tower of London to gasp at the beauty of the magnificent Star of India in the royal scepter, and to gaze in awe at the Black Prince's ruby in the St. Edward's crown which, a guide was explaining, "is worn by each monarch

27

only once in a lifetime—at the moment of coronation." She was fascinated by the diminutive crown, made especially for Queen Victoria "because," the guide said, "she was such a tiny woman that the heavy crowns gave her a headache."

Leaving the glitter of the jewels, Sandy looked around at the bare stone rooms and shivered as she imagined the chill and the ominous clank of metal bolts as they must have resounded in the ears of the famous prisoners held within these thick fortress walls. She thought of Sir Thomas More, of Lady Jane Grey, of Anne Boleyn. It was said that the ghost of the unhappy Anne still could be seen on an occasional walk through the stone passages. But no matter how much Sandy longed to see the lady, she did not put in an appearance that day—probably too many commoners for her royal taste.

But after the fanfare of all the famous spots, Sandy discovered her personal favorite—the Round Pond in Kensington Gardens. She was to return often to what she began to think of as "her" bench, and from which she had a good view of the statue of Peter Pan cavorting there. She loved to watch the children play, tossing balls, sailing model yachts in the pond, feeding the squirrels; and the nannies chatting while their charges dozed in their prams. The flowers were splashes of bright red, yellow, and orange against the sun-dappled green of the grass.

Sandy watched, wondering if she'd ever have children of her own. A little girl in a blue dress and an Alice-in-Wonderland hair style and a boy just slightly younger with black curly hair and snapping dark eyes were the two she'd like to have, she decided. With Brad she might have . . . but she stifled the thought. Brad was Pam's now.

In spite of her unfulfilled longings, she felt wonderfully at peace at the moment. She wished she'd brought her Bible with her; it would be a perfect spot to have her devotions. Instead, looking at the delightful scene around her prompted her to quote her favorite verse to herself, "Delight yourself also in the Lord; and He shall give you the desires of your heart. Commit your way unto the Lord; trust also in Him, and He shall bring it to pass."

Then she frowned, feeling a small cloud pass overhead. How could quoting a Bible verse—especially her favorite—blot the beauty of the moment? She had committed her way to the Lord, and she believed with all her heart that He had something special in store for her. She had to wait for God's perfect timing to bring it about, but no matter how sure her faith, she did get tired of waiting. And she was hurt when something she wanted didn't work out. But she *wasn't* going to think of Brad and Pam.

Her meditations came to an abrupt end as a hissing, spitting golden ball of fur shot in front of her. Following closely was a great flurry of yapping barks, flying feet, and a dragging leash as a brown and white fox terrier dashed by, just a few yards ahead of two little girls in frantic pursuit. Sandy jumped to her feet and joined in the breathless chase. In only a matter of moments, Sandy outdistanced the children and brought the runaway miscreant to an abrupt halt by stamping on the loose red leather leash.

She handed the lead to the taller of the two girls who was already regaining her composure. The child wiped the perspiration from her forehead with the back of her hand, gave a little shake of her head, which caused her well-cut brown hair to fall into place, and looked up at Sandy with round brown eyes. "Thank you ever so much," she said with great solemnity. "Actually, Cinnamon isn't a naughty dog, he was just too eager to catch the cat."

Sandy was enchanted with the child's self-possession. The younger girl, her long blond hair tousled from the race, was still snuffling, but dropped to her knees to bury her face in Cinnamon's short curly hair. "You mustn't do that again, Cinnamon. We mightn't have got you back."

Sandy assured the girls she was delighted to be of service to them and to Cinnamon, and stood smiling after them as they returned in the direction they had come, but in a more orderly fashion. "We got him, Daddy!" The older girl called, and Sandy's heart lurched at the sight of the tall, dark man striding toward the girls. It wasn't Martin, but the similarity was striking. The breeze shifted the branches overhead and a pool of sunlight fell on Sandy. It *was* a beautiful day.

Karen called midweek to say that Bill had booked a room at the Cambridge Inn for them for Saturday night and she would be by at eight o'clock that morning to pick Sandy up.

At twenty minutes past seven, Sandy snapped the lid shut on her overnight bag and took one more look in the clouded mirror over her dresser. At least there was nothing wrong with her looks. This English climate was wonderful for her hair and skin, giving her a Dresden glow she could never achieve with moisture lotions alone. It had been her good fortune to inherit her mother's creamy complexion—although she still remembered her mother's skin as being fabulous while she thought of her own as merely nice.

*Now, however* . . . she thought with a glow of pleasure as she surveyed her appearance, *well, you just might do.* She smiled at the reflection in the mirror, a wide bright smile that revealed the perfectly straight teeth that had cost Aunt Martha all her egg money in orthodontic bills.

Sandy turned away from the mirror and slipped into her jacket. She had chosen her white suit for this special occasion, and the pink blouse

31

with the piecrust ruffled neckline was the perfect color to complement her radiant complexion.

"I have a surprise," said Karen a few minutes later, taking Sandy's bag from her and leading the way to a powerful-looking silver car outside the little hotel.

Before Sandy had a chance to reply, the door on the driver's side of the car opened, and Martin climbed out. *Now why did he have to come?* She took a step backward. *And this was going to be such a nice weekend.*

The day was warm and he was wearing a shirt that looked startlingly white against his tanned skin, especially since the shirt was opened at the neck and the sleeves rolled up. In spite of herself Sandy admired his well-tailored navy blue slacks and the white sweater with red and navy ribbing tied casually around his shoulders. *Maybe without the blazer on, he won't push me around so much,* she thought wryly as he helped her into the front seat of the car.

The powerful motor purred into life almost noiselessly for the amount of energy Sandy could feel pulsating from beneath the hood. "What is it?" she asked, admiring the Morocco leather seats and plush carpet.

"Rolls," Martin replied simply.

"Gorgeous," she said.

Martin gave her an approving smile—the first he'd directed at her. It lit his eyes and creased little lines at their corners. "You, too," he said.

Sandy was flabbergasted. No one had ever said such a thing to her before.

While Karen, leaning eagerly over the back seat, chatted with her brother, Sandy had an opportunity to study the profile of the man sitting beside her. His lean features revealed an aristocratic bone structure with a strength and virility that left no hint of effeteness. Suddenly, in Sandy's mind, it all added up. The woman in the airport, Martin's expensive car, his undeniably dashing good looks, his sudden overture, even his tan—so uncharacteristic for a Londoner—spelled a swinger, a man of the world who collected fast women and fast cars and discarded one as quickly as the other. *No, thank you!*

They drove through a tiny village with a few brick buildings set right by the road and a little pond in the center of the village square, and then they were back out in the rolling countryside again.

"Everything is so *green*," Sandy said, then was embarrassed to discover that she had spoken her thought aloud. It sounded so inane.

But Karen responded warmly, "Yes, isn't it beautiful? Of course, we have to put up with our beastly climate—but I think it's worth it. Look, just beyond those trees, that's the river Cam."

"Already? But we just left London."

"Remember," Martin answered, "England is only about the size of your state of Alabama."

"And just think of all you've given to the

world. I guess Americans tend to equate bigness with greatness, but it isn't necessarily so."

They entered Cambridge on Trumpington Street. Sandy was immediately charmed by the narrow, medieval trafficways, bustling with cars, bicycles, and pedestrians. As Trumpington Street ran into King's Parade, Sandy got her first view of King's College Chapel, its white Gothic spires rising to the sky in an exultation of praise. Sandy felt her own heart filling.

They detoured through a modern shopping district, turned at a corner where an ancient round church stood beneath its conical slate roof, and then the powerful horses of the Rolls came to rest.

"Here we are—Trinity College. Look, there's Bill waiting for us!" Karen jumped out of the car ahead of the others, her eyes on the young man who left his lounging position against the stone wall to walk briskly toward them.

But Sandy's attention was drawn to the great gate of Trinity with the statue of Henry VIII standing commandingly atop. Through the gate she could just glimpse the large stone courtyard with its Renaissance fountain in the center.

Bill's friend, Charles, and Charles's girl friend, Cordelia, would be joining their party. Sandy was only vaguely aware of the formalities of the introduction, her soul feasting on the atmosphere of this storied city of stone and glass, of trees and water, of the past and of the future.

She was brought back to the present as Martin touched her arm, "That rather makes us a pair, it seems. I hope you have no objections."

"What?" Suddenly she realized Bill had been explaining the plans for the day—something about the impossibility of six people along with the picnic gear fitting in one punt. She and Martin—a pair for the day? She could hardly believe it would suit him any more than it did her, but there didn't seem to be any alternative. And she wondered fleetingly why he had come anyway—Karen had probably begged. "Oh, no, of course not, no objections," she stammered, not sounding very convincing.

Martin gave an enigmatic smile at her answer, and she wondered if she were the first woman to refuse to turn handsprings at the suggestion of a day in his company.

But once they were settled in the small, shallow boat and began gliding across the slow, smooth waters of the Cam, Sandy began to think it might not have been such a bad plan after all. Karen and the others made a rather noisy party in the punt just ahead, laughing and calling to friends in passing boats. But Sandy and Martin remained silent, his attention given to his task of propelling the flat-bottomed boat by standing in the stern and pushing on a long pole. Sandy relaxed, warmed by the sun sparkling on the water, and smiled at a comical scene. A mother duck with a string of babies paddling behind her busily herded them to the safety of the riverbank, quacking her commands as the punt passed by. Water skippers danced on the sky, reflected in the surface of the river.

"There's St. John's Bridge up ahead." Martin pointed and Sandy twisted around in her seat. "They call it the Bridge of Sighs."

Sandy nodded. She could see why. She recognized it as a smaller version of its Venetian counterpart. The beautiful, pale stone bridge spanned the river like lacework, its gothic-arched windows filled with delicate tracery. Each of the colleges that backed up to the river boasted a wide lawn sloping down to the water and was connected to the Backs, the grassy parkway which ran most of the length of the university, by its own bridge. Willow trees dipped their spidery boughs in the cool green water. The traffic on Queen's Road beyond the Backs seemed miles— even centuries—away. Sandy felt she could be a Victorian lady on an outing with her swain as easily as a twentieth-century tourist.

Drawing her gaze from the peaceful scene to Martin, she was disturbed to find his eyes resting on her. He looked away quickly before she had a chance to read anything in that look. Was he bored? Contemptuous? Merely curious?

Now it was her turn to watch him and admire the graceful, easy rhythm with which he thrust the pole deep in the river bed, pushed the boat forward, lifted the pole, and repeated the process. The pole often came up dripping and laden with dark green weeds from the depths of the river. Other punters were often thrown off rhythm by this burden, or splashed themselves and their passengers in disengaging their pole, but Martin handled the primitive punt pole with the same masterful control he used on his automobile.

Not for the first time, Sandy felt her curiosity aroused about this mysterious man. Since her initial inauspicious encounters with him, he had not seemed boorish or mannerless, merely distant and withdrawn. What did he *do*? And closer to home, what did he think of *her*? And why was he *here*?

His gaze turned to her again and their eyes met and held. He didn't look away but continued to smile at her warmly—a smile that made her heart contract strangely.

*No*, she thought sharply, *that's the way he smiles at everyone. Don't be so naïve, Sandy.*

# CHAPTER 3

WHEN MARTIN TOOK HER HAND to help her out of
the gently rocking boat, Sandy felt an almost
electric shock. She took a deep breath to control
her sudden impulse to tremble. She was safely
ashore, yet he still held her hand. She wondered
how long her hand would have stayed in that
firm, secure grasp if Karen and Cordelia had not
turned from their punt laden with picnic gear and
Martin had not stepped forward to relieve them
of their burden. Had she really felt a gentle
squeeze before he released his hold?

"This is Midsummer Common," Karen said,
waving her arm in an arc to encompass the
parklike area. "Every Midsummer's Eve there's
a fair here. Has been ever since the Middle Ages,
I guess."

The party settled in a shady spot near the river

38

and Karen began unpacking the baskets. "Oh, Bill, I can't wait to see what you've ordered! It smells divine!"

And indeed it tasted just as divine. A whole roasted chicken, still warm in its foil bag—crisp and brown on the outside, sweet and juicy inside; an enormous loaf of crusty French bread with sweet, lightly salted butter; rich, creamy double Gloucester cheese that melted deliciously on the tongue; small golden French melons more fragrant and juicy than cantaloupes; enormous red, ripe strawberries; a selection of small cakes, some light as sponge, some moist and heavy with fruit and spices; and of course, thermoses of wonderful, fresh tea.

Sandy thought she had never eaten a more delectable meal in a more delectable spot. The branches of a chestnut tree moved gently above her head and at her feet a carpet of tiny yellow-centered white daisies spread across the grass. The breeze ruffled the water, making it lap lightly on the bank, and the sun reflected like diamonds off its broken surface.

It was just possible that Sandy had never eaten in better company. Karen and Bill were a delightful couple, such fun to be with as they chatted and teased, easily sharing their love for each other with those around them. She was enjoying Charles and Cordelia, too, as she became better acquainted with them throughout the meal. There she stopped. She refused to allow her thoughts to dwell on the handsome man sitting so close beside her that their shoulders brushed occasionally. She knew that the scent of his clean, masculine lime aftershave would forever be part of her memory of this day.

"Did you bring your bathing costumes? There's a pool on the green," Charles suggested.

"Oooh, I'm too full. I'd sink," groaned Cordelia.

"How about the Alexandra Gardens?" Bill suggested. "The roses won't be in bloom yet, but the plantings are quite lovely anyway."

"Great!" Karen jumped to her feet, leaving her task of repacking the basket half-finished. "I'll race you to the bridge."

"Run along, children," Martin said, leaning languidly against the trunk of the tall horse chestnut tree. "Sandra and I shall stay right here and guard the leftovers. You're sure to return from your escapade, famished." He spoke lightly, but it was a command.

As the others raced off, their laughter mingling with the sunshine and floating back through the air, Sandy sat very still, her mouth slightly open. "I've seldom been called Sandra."

"You should be; it's a lovely name."

"It sounds lovely the way you say it." He had given it the English pronunciation, as though the name were spelled *Saundra*. "It sounds so . . . well, sophisticated."

"Yes. That suits you."

Her large eyes opened even wider. She couldn't believe her ears. This suave, cosmopolitan man was calling *her* sophisticated? Then she realized what was happening. She must have been right in judging him to be a womanizer. This was his line and he was laying it on with infinite skill. Okay. She would play his game—up to a point. Then he would get a surprise.

So she laughed and replied lightly, "Well, of course! All orphan girls who are reared in Midwest America and who graduate from small New England church colleges and who teach in little Christian schools emerge with a continental sophistication you can't believe."

He frowned at her mockery and seemed to withdraw a little. So this wasn't going according to his scenario? The script had probably called for her to melt on the spot.

"I didn't mean to offend you. Perhaps my word choice was wrong," he studied her for a moment, "although I don't think so. There is something different about you."

*He's really good at this*, Sandy thought. *He sounds caring and genuinely intrigued.* She was glad she had her previous encounters for a mental shield. It would be very easy to be drawn under his spell.

"Of course I'm different. I'm an American."

"I've known dozens of American women, but none like you."

*I'll just bet you have, and English women, and*

41

*French women, and . . . I wonder what he did with his dark charmer today?*

Sandy moved away from him, covering the action by reaching around her to gather a lapful of miniature daisies. She slit a small hole in each two-inch stem and inserted another stem through, forming a daisy chain, as she began a like chain of chatter about her everyday life—her teaching, her summer plans, her long desire to come to England. . . .

If she hadn't been convinced he was simply amusing himself with her, she could have told Martin what was different about her. It was very possible that she was the first woman he had met with a vital faith. Having the assurance that God was in control and that He would direct her gave her life a still point at its center. Her sense of irony did prick her around the edges a bit—just how would he respond to such a statement?

Watching him covertly, she observed that he seemed distinctly irritated by his inability to get close to her. She took secret pleasure in her power and thought, *Well, here's one for all the hearts you've broken. But just don't make a pass at me. I don't want the afternoon spoiled.*

Still—when he looked at her with those piercing, yet gentle warm brown eyes. . . .

"Why is it you always wanted to come to England?"

She finished her daisy chain and slipped it around her forehead like a wreath, thinking about her answer. This was something deeply personal, too; yet something she was willing to share.

She thought a moment longer, then spoke: "For two thousand years Jews have said at every Passover, 'Next year in Jerusalem.' For practically as long as I can remember, I've said every summer, 'Next year in England,' with much the same sense of longing." She paused. "But I really don't know why or where the desire came from. Of course, there was darling little Mr. Hogan, my freshman English teacher in high school who introduced me to Jane Austen; and Mrs. Baker, my senior English teacher, who inspired me to follow in her profession. . . ."

She picked another daisy and twirled it between her fingers. Martin sat silently, as if quietly encouraging her to go on, so she did. "But it must have been inborn, really, because it started much too young to have anything to do with an appreciation of a more gracious way of life, or a sense of history, or any of the things I think of now. What's the word for that?" She frowned, struggling for recall. "Oh, yes, *atavism*."

"Is your family British?"

She shrugged, "Some were—generations back—and some were French, and some German, and some Dutch—which all adds up to solid mix-and-match American. I suppose that somehow accounts in part for our being brash and loud and hurried and all the other negative things we hear about our national character."

43

Martin grinned and shook his head, "You've been listening to the wrong analysts. I find all of you to be open, fresh, self-assured, and utterly charming."

"Do you come into contact with Americans through your work?" she asked, hoping to learn something about him.

But before he could reply, the merrymakers returned from their romp—ravenous, as Martin had predicted. The remains of the picnic were consumed and the empty baskets stowed in the punts. Karen and Bill elected to join Martin and Sandy on the return trip, so the delicate atmosphere between them had no chance to become complicated.

For dinner that evening the two couples drove into the countryside to an old coaching inn that had been modernized and turned into a popular restaurant. The food was excellent—succulent spring lamb with spears of fresh, tender asparagus and a light strawberry mousse—but Sandy felt the modernization intruded on the historic building's rustic charm. And the five-piece orchestra, playing on a raised dais at one side of the room was much too loud.

Twice during dinner Sandy's skin prickled, and she knew Martin's unsettling gaze was on her again. It made for a rather awkward meal, since in the course of the conversation she frequently talked to him, but couldn't trust herself to look directly into those eyes. Her tendency to blush was the price she paid for her fragile complexion, and she hated it—it always made her feel like a wilting heroine on a Victorian fainting couch.

She was further disconcerted by the fact that she was so enchanted by her friends' British accents that she sometimes forgot to concentrate on their words—like listening to a particularly melodious song. She would become mesmerized by the sound, only to realize suddenly that she hadn't comprehended a single word. At least if anyone noticed her lapses, they were too polite to let on.

The red-coated waiter had just served their tea and a plate of mints, when he returned to the table with a message. "There's a call for you, sir," he said to Martin. Sandy had noticed Martin's giving his name to the maître d' when they came in, and was surprised now by the troubled look in Martin's eyes and the tight lines around his mouth as he excused himself.

Conversation continued, but Sandy noticed that several times Karen glanced uneasily from Martin's empty chair to the door. When at last he returned, Karen gave her brother a questioning look. He nodded curtly, but said nothing.

As they were leaving, Bill was hailed by a group of Trinity men at another table. Karen and Bill stepped over to talk to them and came back shortly, saying, "They've invited us all to go on with them. There's a new club just up the road with an orchestra that's even better than this one. Shall we?''

Sandy had been longing to escape to the peace and quiet of the fresh night air and was in no mood to be blasted by an "even better" orchestra. "I hate to be a wet blanket," she began, "but it has been a rather long day—"

Martin cut in, "I think not, thank you, Karen. You and Bill have a good time and I'll see Sandra back to the inn."

It was settled. It seemed that when Martin spoke, that was how things were.

The evening air was cool and Sandy shivered inside her red silk dress in spite of the long full sleeves and flowing skirt. When she got to the car, she was glad she had brought the jacket from her navy blue suit to put around her shoulders. She pulled down the visor and checked her hair as Martin walked around to the other door. She pulled a few soft curls forward on her cheek and noticed how her slim gold necklace and matching earrings caught the glow from the lighted mirror.

"No need to check. I can tell you it's all in very good order," Martin said as he slid under the wheel. "But you don't mind if it gets rumpled just a bit, do you?" He pushed a button and the sun roof slipped back. "It's a shame to let all those stars go to waste." Whatever had caused his earlier anxiety had vanished, and he was now perfectly relaxed.

The car slid smoothly onto the country lane,

and Sandy settled back into the soft cushions. "Mmm, it is a beautiful night. What is that gorgeous scent?"

"Syringa. There's a hedgerow of it just along there." He flicked the high beam of the headlights to catch a row of bushes covered with white blossoms. As Sandy leaned forward for a better look, her jacket slipped from her silk-clad shoulders. She started to reach for it, but Martin was quicker. With a deft motion he slipped the fallen jacket around her shoulders, settled her back against the cushions, and left his arm around her shoulders, his hand cupping her arm gently and moving her just a fraction closer to him in the process.

No matter how sternly she scolded herself, or how hard she argued, she had to admit it felt very nice—very warm and comfortable and secure to have Martin's arm cradling her.

"Anything special you want to do tomorrow?" Martin asked.

Tomorrow? Sunday. "Well, of course I'd like to go to church. . . ."

"Fine, we'll go to King's. You really must hear their choir."

That wasn't quite what Sandy had in mind, but what could she say? Besides, Martin didn't wait for her reply. "I think services are at eleven. I'll pick you up at ten and we can have breakfast first."

Didn't he ever *ask*? But then, after years of

making her own way, it was rather nice to have someone take charge so efficiently. Martin switched on the radio, holding the wheel briefly with his knee, so as not to disturb the arm around Sandy. The sound of soft music floated through the scented night air.

When they arrived back at the inn, they walked slowly through the little flower-bordered garden at the rear, neither seemingly in any hurry to end the evening. Martin led her to an old stone bench that stood in a sheltered spot under the sweeping boughs of a willow. But they never sat down. Just as she was turning toward the bench, Sandy found herself in Martin's embrace. As his head bent toward hers and she felt his breath on her cheek, she found she had no desire to struggle. She felt the pleasant roughness of his tweed jacket and the firmness of his chest next to her own softness. He was so strong, so secure . . . and then he released her abruptly, still supporting her with one arm. A dog barked close behind her and Sandy jumped.

"Good evening," Martin said, as the gardener strolled by, his corgi bounding at his heels.

"Evenin', sir." The gardener tugged at his cap in respectful greeting. "Beautiful evenin', ma'am."

Sandy murmured her agreement, but she knew much of the beauty had disappeared.

## CHAPTER 4

THE NEXT MORNING SANDY AWOKE to the pealing of church bells. She lay, only half awake, between her soft cotton flannel sheets, wondering why she was so happy. She could feel her heart swelling in her chest and she had the most unreasonable desire to dance around the room and sing.

Her first Sunday in England—and she was to worship in one of the most famous churches in the world. With that thought, she leaped out of bed and splashed water on her face at the small basin in her room. She slipped into her navy blue suit and lime-green blouse and turned to brush her hair. Then she froze. No hat! Would one be required in an Anglican service? That question opened up a whole Pandora's box of nervous thoughts—what else might be required of her?

Until that moment she had not realized what a sheltered spiritual existence she had lived, never having attended any church but those of the small, fundamentalist denomination Aunt Martha had reared her in. Even the college she attended and the private school where she taught were amazingly similar. She hadn't consciously turned her back on opportunities for wider experience; they simply hadn't presented themselves before.

Well, today would change that.

At five minutes to ten she went down to the tiny lobby of the Cambridge Inn to wait for Martin. He could be rude and mannerless, and certainly his playboy way of toying with her was obvious, but she couldn't wait to see him.

She sat on the tapestry-upholstered sofa, leafing through a well-worn issue of *Country Life*. Sandy glanced at the pictures of Georgian country estates and Victorian town houses offered for sale, but concentration was impossible. Her eyes constantly sought the doorway for his entrance; her ears were attune to the sound of his powerful car on the pavement.

She glanced at her watch. Only five after. It seemed as though she'd been waiting hours. Tossing the magazine aside, she walked to the door to look up and down the street. The glorious sunshine of yesterday was making a valiant struggle to break through a cheerless cloud cover. Here and there a golden ray triumphed, but it was too soon to predict which would win out.

Sandy sighed with impatience and began the confined activity of pacing around the small lobby. *Oh, I forgot my Bible!* Perfect. She'd run up to her room and get it and come down again. Martin would never know she'd been waiting so impatiently.

She flew up the two flights of stairs to her room, picked up the leather-bound volume by her bedside, checked her hair and make-up again in the mirror, and hurried back down, sure that Martin would be there. The lobby was empty.

With a sigh of frustration she sank down on the sofa. Well, she could read her Bible. The pages fell open easily to her favorite passage, Psalm 37:4: " . . . and He shall give you the desires of your heart. . . ."

She smiled at the familiar words. She had quoted them in the park only a few days ago, and it seemed these words were becoming the motto of her trip. The Lord had certainly granted her heart's desire in this long-awaited trip to England, but what of her other desires? She sighed and closed the book. That she believed the promises of the Scripture didn't change the fact that she was still dealing with an annoying number of human frustrations. Would love and companionship continue to elude her?

The tread of a masculine foot on the tile floor brought her bolt upright. But as she sprang from her chair, the smile died on her lips. The hotel manager put an envelope in her hand. "Miss Hollis, a young gentleman came by early this morning and asked me to give this to you."

Sandy was furious with herself for trembling as she tore open the crested vellum paper.

Dear Sandra,

Sorry about our date. I'm off to London—Emergency. Will call you later.

Martin

The words of the hurried scrawl in the heavy black ink blurred before her eyes. She crumpled the stiff paper into a tight ball.

Was he running out on her? Or on the prospect of being roped into attending church? He hadn't objected last night, but one of his apparent lifestyle could hardly be expected to be an ardent churchgoer. Well, either way, it was obvious that, to him, her company wasn't worth the price of sitting through a church service. Fortunate for her that she had learned the truth—or rather, had her suspicions reconfirmed—before she found herself in another embrace like last night—enjoying it even more.

So much for Mr. Martin Graham. But there was certainly no reason for her to change her plans just because he had bolted.

It was too late now for breakfast, so Sandy marched down King's Parade beside the high wrought-iron ornamental screen that bordered the college lawn. It looked as though the clouds were dominating the sky and threatening a drizzle, but she didn't bother about an umbrella. She was too furious to think of one.

Sandy knew she had no one but herself to blame for her disappointment. From her first sight of him, or rather of his beastly arm flung in her face, she had been suspicious of Martin and his escapades. How could she possibly expect anything better from him than that he would stand her up? *And before breakfast, too. Changed his mind in the middle of the night and took a flyer. Emergency—I'll just bet! If only I hadn't let him put his arm around me.* The memory of his aborted embrace flooded her mind, her cheeks staining red at the thought. *And you like it,* she chided herself. *You wanted more—you know you did. It serves you right.* Scolding herself didn't make her feel any better.

What did make her feel better, however, was the pealing of the church bells that broke out right above her head, calling worshippers to service. And her heart soared like the vaulted ceiling as she entered the great church. She slipped quickly into a pew in the nave, feasting on the creations of artists and craftsmen seeking to glorify God with their skill. In spite of overcast skies, the stained-glass windows glowed with the radiance of rare jewels, their crimsons, blues, greens and golds glowing richly. As her gaze was drawn upward to the spreading fans of white stone, so, too, were her spirits. How silly to be so disturbed over Martin. After all, he was nothing to her. She was perfectly accustomed to attending church alone, and she could worship just as well without him. Better, no doubt. She began to feel more at ease, in spite of the fact that most of the other women were, indeed, wearing hats.

Sandy was admiring the intricate hand carving of the ornate wooden rood screen when the voices of the choirboys filled the church with the clear, treble music of Vivaldi's *Gloria* : 'Glory be to God on high . . . We praise thee, We bless thee, We glorify thee . . . '' Sandy was engulfed with a sense of the greatness and omnipotence of God in a way she had never known before. ''We give thee thanks for thy great glory.'' But as the final notes echoed from the vaulted ceiling, she suddenly felt uneasy—what was she doing *here* on a Sunday morning? Her earlier misgivings returned and she felt she should have found a small chapel where she could be singing ''Amazing Grace.''

The first lesson was read by the presiding clergyman, and the General Confession followed. Sandy stood and groped for the Prayer Book from the pew rack in front of her. She wanted to respond with the congregation—but what page were they on? The lady standing next to her handed her an open book and Sandy smiled her thanks and joined in the reading: "Almighty and most merciful Father, we have erred and strayed from thy ways, like lost sheep. We have followed too much the devices and desires of our own hearts. We have . . . "

The words were fine—precisely in accord with the teaching of Scripture and her basic theology class at college—but could they have the same effect when they were read, rather than coming spontaneously from the heart? She despised herself for being critical—yet this was so different, so foreign from anything she had experienced.

Communion, or Eucharist as they called it, came next. And again Sandy struggled: Did their rules require membership in that church to take the sacrament? What if she went to the altar and was refused? But wouldn't staying in her seat be denying her relationship with God? As the others in her pew rose, Sandy stood, too—no one was looking at her but God, and He knew her heart was right before Him.

"This is the cup of My body . . . This do in remembrance of Me . . ." the minister quoted. Sandy drank, in that moment of worship, not even thinking about the fact that the wine was served in a communal cup.

When all had returned to their seats, the minister mounted the pulpit to the left of the chancel before Rubens's magnificent "Adoration of the Magi" that served as an altarpiece, and preached a brief sermon. Later, though, Sandy was unable to remember the subject. Her mind was too busy trying to sort out the experience. So this was the way Martin worshiped—if he did—maybe at Christmas or Easter or to please his sister. It certainly wasn't a bit like the dear, familiar fellowship of Aunt Martha's square red brick building with the cross on top, or her own little white steepled village church, but it did have a beauty and majesty that made it easy to believe that "The Holy One of Israel is among you in majesty."

Was such a service equally pleasing to God? Had her own notions of a *real* Christian church been . . . well—not wrong, but too small? Had she limited God to her narrow perception of Him? Of course, it wasn't really the style of church or the form of worship that mattered anyway, but what was in one's heart—and she was afraid she knew all too well what was in Martin Graham's heart.

Packing, back in her room, Sandy opened the door to Karen's knock. "Hullo. Did you have a nice morning?"

Sandy smiled and nodded. As it turned out, she had.

"I'm afraid I slept in," Karen yawned and stretched, "We got in beastly late last night, but it was fun. Anyway, I've come to tell you that Bill will be driving us back to London. Martin

had to leave early this morning. Did you know?''
At Sandy's nod, she continued, "It's a shame,
but it can't be helped. It happens quite often."

Sandy wasn't a bit surprised. Unreliability
could now be added to the list of Martin Graham's doubtful charms. And if Karen knew
anything more about the enigma, it was clear she
was keeping her own counsel.

Sandy briefly considered confiding what she
knew about the situation to Karen. But as much
as she liked Karen, she still felt she must keep
her at a distance. She didn't want another friend
who could betray her as Pam had.

The door clicked as Karen left the room.
Sandy looked up with a jerk—not startled by the
closing door, but by her own thought. *Betrayal?*
Was that really how she felt about Pam? She had
never taken it out and looked at it. She had
impassively refused to dwell on what had happened. Pam was her friend and, when Pam and
Brad fell in love, she stoically submerged her
own feelings and refused to consider them.

But then there was really nothing to consider,
was there? Jealousy wasn't an acceptable emo-
tion for a Christian, so she had to be happy for
Pam. And that was that. But she didn't have to
let anyone else in the places Pam and Brad had
occupied—places close to her heart where they
could hurt her. She would thank Karen and Bill
for the weekend and then go on with her

itinerary. After all, there really was no reason she should see any of them again. Ever.

Sandy's week was full: Monday, Westminster Abbey and the Houses of Parliament; Tuesday, Harrod's and a walking tour of Dickens's London; Wednesday, Osterley House.

But this morning, before she again tested her growing skill in getting around by subway—the *tube*, she corrected—she would sleep just a little longer. She turned over lazily, relishing the luxury. No school bells to answer, no papers to grade, no lessons to plan—just her own delicious time to do whatever she wanted. And what she wanted at the moment was to lie in bed. The fabled slower pace of English life could become addictive.

A rap at the door interrupted her indolence. "Yes?" she called.

"Telephone for you in the lobby, Miss."

She groaned and hastily pulled on some clothes. Next to mixer faucets, the amenity she missed most was the American custom of a phone in every room, even in an inexpensive hotel.

"Hello?"

"Hello. Sandra? You sound sleepy. Don't you know it's the middle of the day?" The voice was lightly mocking and, even over the phone, its note of command and assurance was palpable.

"I've called to see if I've been forgiven for Sunday."

"There's nothing to forgive, Martin. Really," she replied coolly.

"Ouch! I think I just got frostbitten."

"Sorry, I guess I'm not really awake yet." What did he expect her to say?

"Well, I want an opportunity to make it up to you. Will you let me take you to Winchester for your pilgrimage this weekend? Leave Friday afternoon?"

Sandy drew in her breath and her mind whirled. She couldn't possibly answer over this public phone.

"Sandra? Are you there? You haven't gone back to sleep, have you?"

"No. I mean, yes, Martin, I'm here. But I couldn't possibly. I mean, thank you for asking and all that but. . . ."

"Are you still that angry with me?" he sounded hurt. "I really couldn't help it, Sandra."

"No, no. It isn't that at all."

"Have you made other plans? Couldn't they be changed? I can't get away just any weekend."

"Martin, I don't want to offend you, but I can't explain over the phone. I'm sorry."

"Okay, then, how about tea? Could you explain over tea?"

She surrendered. "I don't know that I can explain at all, but I'll try."

"Fine. I'll pick you up at two."

Back in her room Sandy was still hearing his voice and the click of the receiver over and over in her mind. She opened the small closet and surveyed the clothing possibilities. Her selection didn't fill even this tiny cubbyhole. The choices had seemed limitless when her wardrobe was being planned, but now it was so important to look right—especially since Martin seemed to notice everything. After long deliberation and checking to be sure the sun was shining, she chose the apricot voile.

As the dress slipped over her head, the deep ruffle around the neckline floated over her shoulders and the skirt fell around her legs in graceful folds. If only her words could flow as naturally.

She had just picked up her leather clutch bag when the manager's wife knocked at her door. "There's a gentleman 'ere for you, dearie." Sandy opened the door. "Oh, and don't you look ever so lovely. 'Ave a good time, I'm sure." Sandy returned her smile with appreciation.

The woman's words sent her down the stairs on a note of assurance, but she felt her confidence declining when she saw Martin standing by the hotel desk, watching her. She took a deep breath, lifted her chin just a trifle, and forced a bright smile.

One look at Martin took her breath away. Dressed with his usual attention to detail, he wore a dark blue vested suit with a pale yellow shadow-striped shirt. His necktie was a rich, subtle pattern of blue and gold diagonal stripes, and he had a pale yellow silk handkerchief in his breast pocket.

They exchanged greetings and he offered his arm. Sandy slipped her hand through the crook in his elbow, and they went out into the early summer afternoon. "Ready for tea?" he asked.

Sandy laughed. "I should have warned you—I haven't even had breakfast yet."

"Wonderful! You'll love this."

"Where are we going?"

"It's a surprise. Hold tight." She wished he'd quit smiling at her with one eyebrow raised like that. She needed to keep her mind on the purpose of this outing.

To Sandy's surprise Martin directed the Rolls toward the Thames and the Houses of Parliament. "I didn't know there was a tea shop in the area."

"A very exclusive one." He raised his eyebrow at her again as he parked in a numbered spot practically in the shadow of Big Ben, then came around to open her door for her.

Martin escorted her through the wood-paneled, marble-floored halls that had so impressed her on her tour earlier in the week. But somehow they seemed even more magnificent today. And she was immensely interested by the number of people who greeted Martin as they made their way to the sweeping, oak-banistered stairway in the interior of the building.

The smooth worn places in the marble stairs made Sandy wonder how many thousands of feet through how many hundreds of years had worn those swales? And whose feet? In her mind she could see Charles I charging into the House of Commons to arrest its members; Lord North, hurrying to advise Parliament to pass the Stamp Act; Disraeli, en route to have Queen Victoria declared Empress of India.

Another paneled hallway, this one floored in black and white terrazzo squares, led them to a pair of high, paneled doors with heavy brass fittings. The doorman standing at attention gave Martin a smile of recognition and immediately stepped aside to open the doors for them. Sandy had the feeling he was going to bow to them, but he merely smiled and nodded again as they passed through. If only she didn't have such an unpleasant conversation ahead of her, she would be loving every minute of this.

The elegant dining room was richly furnished, with thick red plush carpeting, dark wood, and the gleam of silver and crystal. One windowed wall overlooked the Thames.

"On the terrace this afternoon, I think, Manning," Martin said to the headwaiter, resplendent in white tie and tails.

"Very good, sir. It is quite lovely today."

They were led across the busy, but hushed

room, through an ornately paneled door and onto a stone-flagged terrace set with tables, the appointments sparkling in the sun. Well-groomed bushes grew in pots along the side, and beyond the stone balustrade flowed the Thames, choked with traffic.

"Oh, Martin, what a delightful surprise! It's lovely." As she spoke, a gentle breeze from the river ruffled the light fabric of her dress. Martin murmured his agreement, but he wasn't looking at the river.

The waiter held a chair for her at the flower-decked table sheltered by a canopy. "Set tea today, sir?" The waiter bowed his exit at Martin's nod. He had no more than left the terrace when two waiters in white jackets and black bow ties appeared, bearing trays of tea, tiny cucumber and asparagus sandwiches, thin slices of buttered bread, a beautiful pink cake, and a crystal bowl of the largest strawberries Sandy had ever seen. The cream accompanying the berries was so thick it would hardly leave the pitcher.

"Devonshire cream," Martin explained. "I'm not sure why, but that's the way it is there. Must be something the cows eat—although the grass is the same color in Devon as anywhere else."

Sandy poured the tea and then sat sipping it contentedly as she watched the busy river. Barges, sightseeing cruises, fishing boats, yachts, sailboats—all slipped by in a bustle of business.

"You have shown me a side of England I would never have seen on a schoolteacher's budget, Martin. Thank you, and you must thank your influential friends who made it possible.'"

Martin smiled that enigmatic smile of his, "Oh, I'll be sure to do that. I know a few. Enough to get by."

Again, he was evading her intended question. How could she find out more about him? Perhaps a direct approach was best.

"Martin, what exactly do you do?"

He shrugged, "I work at Whitehall. Just one of a hundred thousand government employees. Push paper, mostly. Spend the taxpayers' money."

Somehow his rugged physique and tanned skin did not match the description of someone who spent his days in a musty government office, but she let it go. Just another of Martin's mysteries. Besides, after she told him what she'd come to say, it wouldn't matter anyway. This encounter would definitely settle things between them.

Sandy chatted about her week—seeing T. S. Eliot's and Rudyard Kipling's graves in Westminster Abbey, visiting the Olde Curiosity Shop and the Cheshire Cheese yesterday. She had no desire to ruin these delectable sandwiches and unbelievable strawberries with a distasteful topic. Martin seemed to sense her feelings and refrained from pressing her further about the weekend.

But finally it could be postponed no longer. She simply couldn't hold another strawberry, and she had run out of banter. She poured herself a third cup of tea, refilled Martin's cup, sighed softly, and prayed fervently, if silently: *Lord, help me!* It all seemed so easy, so cut and dried when she planned what she would say back in her hotel. But now, here, with the sun and the river and Martin sitting just across the small table from her. . . .

"I think you said you had something to tell me," he prompted gently, leaning forward encouragingly, his whole attention on her. "Just why can't you possibly go to Winchester this weekend?"

"Because I won't sleep with you," she blurted. Far from the graceful speeches she had planned, the words hung in the air, gauche and childish. She felt Martin stiffen across from her, but she couldn't look at him. Instead, she sat, staring unseeing at her plate. All the blood in her veins, it seemed, was pouring into her face in one hot flush.

The crashing tension between them was broken by the waiter coming to clear away the dishes. All the time he was there Sandy held her pose, not trusting herself to lift her eyes.

After an interminable time the waiter asked, "Will there be anything else, sir?"

"No, thank you." Martin signed the bill and they were alone again.

Then, to Sandy's utter amazement and confusion, Martin began laughing. "Sandra, you are a darling. I didn't expect such directness, even from an American. Is that really what you thought? I'm surprised you'd speak to me at all. But what have I done to make you think such a thing?"

Martin's laughter eased the tension and Sandy was able to talk again, the fiery blush receding from her face. "Well, you *said* the weekend and I just assumed that was part of the bargain. It seems to be the standard thing these days. . . ." She thought fleetingly of inserting something more personal about her opinion of his standards, but quickly abandoned that idea. " . . . But it's not my standard. I know that must seem incredibly Victorian, but there it is." She put her napkin on the table with a gesture of finality. "The tea has been lovely, thank you."

"Hold on a minute. There it *isn't*. Not at all. My invitation was and is with no strings attached. Do you want a character reference from my vicar? I do have one, you know—a vicar, that is. Separate rooms, separate hotels, if you like. Give me a chance, Sandra."

She couldn't believe what she was hearing. Martin Graham wasn't commanding, wasn't ordering; he was asking, even pleading. She smiled at him, daring to look into his eyes for the first time that day.

# CHAPTER 5

TWO DAYS LATER, still not quite sure how it happened, and certainly not willing to admit to herself how glad she was that it had, Sandy found herself seated in the sleek, silver Rolls, heading southwest of London through the rolling green countryside.

Sandy looked down at her lap and was glad she had chosen to wear her beige skirt and ivory silk shirt today. The shirt's French cuffs and front tucking with her gold jewelry and bone accessories gave her a distinctly refined look in perfect keeping with her companion's attire.

She was enjoying her quiet contemplation of the scenery passing the window when Martin asked, "Say, would you like to see a piece of American soil?"

"Sure," she laughed, "have you got some in a bottle?"

Martin took a road bearing slightly west. "Runnymede. There is an acre of English ground there given to the United States by the people of Britain in memory of John F. Kennedy."

"Oh, yes, I've seen pictures of a white marble monument that says something about that. I'd love to go there."

Martin parked the car and they walked across the flat green meadow beside the Thames surrounded by a verdant growth of trees and bushes, toward the monument on a small hill. "And somewhere here, perhaps under your very feet, is the spot where the Englishman's individual rights of liberty were born." Martin moved his arm in an arc to encompass the field.

Sandy looked at the ground beneath her feet. "Yes, and the American's, too, remember. The Magna Charta gave birth to our Bill of Rights as well. If I remember my American history correctly, those statements of freedom were insisted on by the founding fathers precisely because they had always been the rights of Englishmen— whether in the old world or the new."

"You have present-day support for that sentiment, too." Martin led her to another memorial, this in the style of a classical temple, built by members of the American Bar Association as a tribute to "Freedom under Law."

"And what's up there?" Sandy asked, walking toward a third monument at the top of the hill.

"The Air Forces Memorial from World War II."

When they were standing in front of it, Sandy started to read aloud: "Here are recorded the names of 20,456 airmen who have no known grave. They died for freedom in raid and sortie over the British Isles. . . ." She choked and could read no more. "I'm sorry. One thing I didn't inherit with my Anglophilism was a stiff upper lip."

Martin smiled his warm, amused, understanding smile, "Don't worry about it. Mum never developed that either."

"Oh, I'd forgotten. Karen did tell me your Mother was an American. How did your parents meet?"

"At Oxford. She came over to do a year of study and fell in love with the country before she ever met Dad. He always teased her that the only reason she married him was because her visa was about to expire."

Sandy laughed, "I've heard of worse motives."

She turned from the memorial to the magnificent view of Windsor Castle, with its great round tower. The sun was warm on her face and there was a fresh green scent in the air. The words seemed to be pulled from deep within her: "This happy breed of men, this little world; This precious stone set in the silver sea, Which serves it in the office of a wall, Or as a moat defensive to a house, Against the envy of less happier lands; This blessed plot, this earth, this realm, this England.''

Only at the end did she choke. "I can't believe I got through that without crying. It's always been a favorite of mine, but it suddenly seemed so appropriate with the war memorial here and all. What a shame the silver sea can no longer serve as wall or moat. . . .'' Her voice trailed off as her mind filled with images of earlier, simpler days.

Martin, too, was silent, looking at her strangely, as if trying to evaluate her words. "How odd that you should say that." Then almost abruptly he took her arm and led her across the grass to the banks of the river. There was a refreshing smell of fresh water mint being trodden underfoot as they walked along, watching the unhurried pace of cabin cruisers and small river craft, a restful contrast to the bustle of traffic on the main road less than a hundred yards away.

Only when they were back in the car and once more on the main road to Winchester did it dawn on Sandy that she hadn't actually seen the plot of American soil. Then another marker attracted her attention. "Chawton! Did that sign say Chawton? Oh, Martin, we must stop there, too."

He smiled indulgently, "Anything you say. But why?"

"Chawton cottage. That's where Jane Austen lived after her father's death. Maybe it'll be open. We can stop, can't we?" Her eyes were shining and she sat forward on her seat.

"Oh, yes—Jane. I'd forgotten."

"Forgotten! Then why did you think we'd come?"

Martin didn't reply, instead giving her a long look, one eyebrow raised.

"Martin—watch the road."

They purposely parked outside the village so they could enter it on foot. "As Jane would have," Sandy said.

But in all the time a lonely, impressionable teenage girl had spent dreaming over *Persuasion* and *Mansfield Park* and mentally walking country lanes with Elizabeth Bennett and her sisters, no image ever conjured up could come close to matching this moment. Great fleecy clouds rolled lazily across the blue overhead and the hedgerows were full of twittering birds that seldom showed themselves; the pastures fed mild-faced cows that looked at them with wide-open eyes over stone walls; towering elm trees swayed their branches in the breeze. . . .

"Martin, just think—the clouds and the blue sky, the hedgerows and the birds, the cows and the trees are all just as Jane Austen knew them— no change in almost two hundred years! Isn't it wonderful!" In her excitement she hurried ahead of him, then turned back, her face glowing with

71

the delight of discovery. "See, these stone walls must have stood here then—and those low slate-roofed barns, too—and even that whitewashed cottage. Look, most likely roses grew over the doors just like that when Jane lived here."

Sandy stopped before a snug little cottage. Two perfect rows of flowers lined the little pathway made of coal cinders and leading from gate to cottage door. The flower beds were marked off by pieces of broken crockery set on edge, and the doorway was surrounded by yellow roses. "It's too absolutely storybook to be believed," Sandy laughed. "I'll bet somebody's grandmother lives there."

Martin took Sandy's hand and led her down the street, a tolerant smile playing around his lips, rather in the attitude of an indulgent father taking his favorite child on an outing.

It wasn't at all difficult to locate their goal. A brass plate on the wall identified the two-storied brick house right beside the road as the home of Jane Austen. They entered the gate of the brick wall and walked the stone path through the old-fashioned country garden. Marigolds, daisies, and cosmos grew in profusion, each bedded by height, building to impressive stalks of blue, pink, and white delphinium along the wall.

The house was indeed open. " . . . And here is the general sitting room where she did so much of her writing, subject to all kinds of casual interruptions. But Miss Austen was careful that her occupation should not be suspected by servants or visitors, so she wrote on small sheets of paper that could easily be put away or covered with a piece of blotting paper.'' They were led through the house by a pale lady of indefinite age. Her hair was pale blond, her skin pale ivory, her dress pale blue; but her pale eyes shone when she pointed out the little mahogany writing desk where Elizabeth Bennett, Emma Woodhouse, and Anne Elliott had been born.

Sandy sighed with satisfaction; Martin stifled a yawn. Sandy caught just the end of his action, *Well, I warned him,* she thought.

It was early evening when they came into view of Winchester's red brick buildings, steep rooflines, and tall chimney pots mingling with leafy green trees. Sandy, who had never taught a unit on Anglo-Saxon literature without dreaming of this moment of her triumphal entry into the city, could recite her lecture notes verbatim. This was the ancient city that had so often taken a lead in English history since the days when invading Romans found a powerful Celtic tribe in occupation of the site and set about Romanizing them and setting up defense works. Then the Saxons made Winchester the principal seat of the High King of all England—a position it was not to yield to London until late in the eleventh century.

But their unscheduled stops had brought them to the city later in the day than they had planned.

While Martin checked in at The George, Sandy sat in the conservatory surrounded by mellow wicker furniture, pots of ferns and ivy, and window boxes filled with geraniums. She admired the carpeted white-painted stairs rising to a balustraded .gallery at the far end. When the registration process was complete, it was too late to visit the Cathedral. Sandy swallowed her impatience. She had waited years—a few more hours wouldn't hurt.

They had dinner in a half-timbered inn, which in its long history had been burned down and rebuilt at least three times, always apparently without the aid of plumb lines or levels. The floor sloped so steeply at one point that Sandy almost stumbled, and Martin grasped her arm to steady her. His hand was strong and comforting and Sandy suddenly felt compelled to lean against the man beside her. Shaking off the alarming impulse, she moved away from him.

Sandy gave her attention to the menu and chose Dover sole in mornay sauce, with tiny spring peas as her main course. Sandy had not seen the frown that crossed Martin's rugged features when she had pulled away, but he was still looking stern as he sat across the candle-lit table from her.

"You're awfully quiet. I hope you aren't regretting the bargain," she said in an attempt to break the ice.

Shaking his head, he offered lightly, "I just

wish you'd relax, Sandra. You can trust me. I want the pleasure of your companionship—even fully clothed."

Sandy's laugh belied her thought. *I'm not worried about trusting you. It's myself I don't trust.*

By the time they had finished their trifle, which managed to be rich yet light at the same time, she had relaxed perceptibly. They walked slowly along the streets of Winchester and through a small green park set on a hill where, at the very top, they found a bench beside the path. The late evening air was cool, and Martin put his arm around her and drew her to him. As always, at his touch, Sandy's heart began beating wildly, but she remained outwardly composed, determined not to become another in his string of conquests to be cast aside when someone more interesting appeared on the horizon—as Sandy had no doubt someone would.

At the same time, she was fighting a desperate battle with herself. Being close to him, feeling his warmth, the strength of his arm around her, she longed for more—longed to feel his lips on hers as she so nearly had that night in Cambridge.

"Sandra . . ." Martin began and she could feel his arm tighten around her.

"Hmm?" She looked up at him. His look was one she had never seen before, even from him, not erotic, but far deeper, as though he could look into her very soul. Her face must have registered the shock she felt to see this, for he looked away quickly.

To cover the ensuing silence, Sandy requested, "Tell me more about your American mother."

"Since Dad died she has lived very much in retirement mostly in a small family place in Kent. Karen and I get down to see her as often as our work will permit. Rosegrowing is her great passion. . . ." They went on with their pleasant, getting-to-know-you conversation, but Sandy felt they were both strained—determined to keep it light.

It was getting late by the time they started down the narrow path through the park. Sandy paused to draw in a deep breath of the fresh clean scent of the grass and the sweet aroma of the borders of flowers beyond the path. Then, before the breath was completed, she found herself being pulled tenderly but firmly into Martin's arms. This time there was no interrupting gardener's footfall to break the spell. As his lips closed over hers Sandy began to feel her head spin, and she lost all contact with time and space. She and Martin, his arms enfolding her and his lips caressing her, were all that existed. It was even hard to isolate the touch of his lips and of his body pressed against hers because her whole being was caught up in the experience—the whirling, soaring timelessness.

And then his arms tightened, drawing her even closer to him. His lips were hard and urgent on hers and she responded in a way she hadn't thought possible.

She wanted it to go on and on, the intoxication never to end, but at length his arms relaxed and she rested her head against his chest. *Could this mean so much to me and only be an idle flirtation for him?* her spinning mind questioned. Surely such an experience had to be mutual to have such depth. But with how many women had he shared such a moment? Such exquisite technique spoke of experience. A pair of dark, enigmatic eyes from the airplane swam before her mind's eye, and she pulled away slightly.

"It's getting late," she murmured. Not another word was spoken between them as they walked back to The George, but Martin's arm stayed around her possessively, his hand resting lightly on her waist, his kiss lingering on her lips.

# CHAPTER 6

WALKING DOWN HIGH STREET the next morning, Sandy simply could not understand why she couldn't glimpse the square Norman tower of the cathedral above the tops of the trees? "Are you *sure* this is the right way?"

Martin shook his head and grinned. "Americans are so impatient."

Leaving High Street, they turned up a narrow passage, then walked along an elm-lined lane. Still no glimpse of it. She might be an impatient American, but surely, there was never such a retiring cathedral. And then they were through the dark archway that opened off High Street beyond the obscuring trees, and the immense mass appeared, sprawling over the ground like some stranded prehistoric monster.

"Oh! It's so *plain!*" Sandy couldn't mask the

disappointment in her voice. "It's huge, but plain." She surveyed the enormous bulk of blank wall. No statues or carved work, no spires, towers, pinnacles, or balustrades—only walls, windows, and buttresses.

"Ugliness, like beauty, my dear, is only skin-deep. Inside is one of the finest naves in the country."

And Martin was right. "Oh!" And this time her voice was not tinged with disappointment, but near reverence. "It's like being in a forest of giants." Sandy stood at the back of the two-hundred-fifty-foot aisle and looked up at the sweeping arches, which were nearly as many feet above her head. Rows of columns marched down each side of the nave, indeed looking like mighty trees, their spreading fans interlocking like graceful branches high overhead.

They stood silently for several minutes, Sandy completely taken out of herself, as her heart leapt up to praise her Creator. "I'd like to pray," she said softly. Taking her hand, Martin led her to the Lady Chapel behind the high altar and knelt quietly beside her, while she silently poured out the joys and fears of her heart—joys for the moment; fears for the future. After a few minutes she rose with her face shining.

Wordlessly Martin drew her into his arms and held her. It was a moment of intense sweetness. There were no overtones of passion, and he made no move to kiss her, but she felt closer to him in that interval than at any other time. She wanted to stay there forever, suspended in that hallowed moment.

"Let's go find Jane," Martin said softly, his lips near her cheek, as if afraid the fragile atmosphere would splinter if he spoke aloud.

Sandy startled. She had forgotten all about her reason for coming. "Oh, I meant to bring flowers," she said, her forehead furrowed with regret. "I don't suppose there's a florist shop near?"

Martin smiled indulgently. "Well, we can try."

What they found was far better than a florist shop—a charming old-fashioned garden surrounding a neat white cottage just a few blocks from the cathedral. On the close-clipped lawn, a little girl was playing with a kitten.

They chatted with the child for a few minutes, then Martin inquired, "Is your mum at home? We'd like to buy some flowers from her garden."

The little girl ran around the side of the house, her kitten in her arms, "Mummy!" she called.

In a few minutes a friendly young woman in slacks and a print blouse had filled their arms with delicate sprays of baby's breath, deep blue gentians, and pink and yellow cosmos. She refused payment, delighted to share the abundance of her labors, although she looked just a bit confused when Sandy explained that they were for Jane Austen—"For her grave, you know."

Sandy stood above the plain black marble slab in the floor of the north side of the cathedral. Her floral offering lay just below the simple carved name. Sandy thought of the hours of delight this quiet English maiden lady had brought to her own often dreary life through the pages Jane Austen had filled with her magic. In many ways Sandy owed this trip to Jane, for without the inspiration of her novels would a girl from midwest America ever have developed such reverence for her Anglican heritage? "Thank you, Jane," Sandy whispered, her heart choking her.

And then she looked at the man beside her. He seemed so at home in the magnificence of the cathedral—so secure in his heritage of dignity and peace. He still held some flowers pressed on him by the kitten-girl's mum. "For you," he held them out to Sandy. "Jane would want to share."

"And now, my learned friend, I have a surprise for you!" They stood just outside the cathedral. Martin smiled at her and again Sandy felt the thrill of his eyes shining on her like the sunshine. "Did you know you are within walking distance of the original Round Table of fable and legend?"

"No! You're teasing me, aren't you? I thought no one knew for sure if it even existed."

"Well, come judge for yourself." He offered his arm and led her down a little street. She nestled one hand in the crook of his elbow, feeling the muscles beneath the lightweight linen sport jacket, her other hand gladly clasping the delicate bouquet he had given her, and Sandy knew she had never been happier in her life.

*Why can't I just give myself to this precious moment and quit worrying about the future?* she wondered. *After all, so long as I know it's just a passing thing with him, I'll be prepared for the letdown and I won't be hurt too much.* It was all very logical, but she knew it wasn't true. And then, when he looked down at her and smiled—a smile that combined ardor and kindness and crinkled the little lines at the corners of his eyes—she knew there was no use fighting it, however painful the end would be.

In a few moments they were standing in the great hall of William the Conqueror's castle, looking down a long vista of dark marble columns. And on the wall in front of them was indeed the top of an enormous round table. "Well, what do you think?"

"It's marvelous!" Sandy surveyed the huge weathered oak disc thoughtfully. "And really, what difference does it make whether it's the real one or not? After all, the ideals of peace and justice and brotherhood that it symbolizes are the reality." She turned back to Martin. "But what do the experts think?"

He shrugged doubtfully, "Most don't date it earlier than the thirteenth century. But Henry VII, who favored the Arthurian romance for political reasons, had these figures of all the knights painted round the rim. It does add a certain poetic quality, don't you think?"

"Oh, yes, I must buy postcards of this. It'll mean so much to my students when I teach *Morte d'Arthur* this fall."

"Do you enjoy your teaching, Sandra?"

"I try to pass my love of literature on to my students. You know, a teacher's excitement about a subject is the best way to create enthusiasm in the kids. But I don't just give them literature—we do the history and the art and the music—the whole essence of each period, so they can step back into that time and really put their feet down—the ones who really care, that is."

"Do they? Care, I mean?"

"Some do. I don't kid myself—most are there because English Lit is required. But there are always a few bright lights. Sometimes I think I'm repaying the teachers who inspired me—you know, passing the torch or something."

Martin nodded silently.

After lunch they amused themselves poking around in antique shops. Sandy was surprised and impressed with the knowledge Martin revealed of period furniture, antique silver and china, and paintings. As always he was so observant she found it slightly unnerving—wondering what those quiet deep eyes were seeing.

She noticed that he could recall the name of an

obscure artist long after they had passed by the painting, or could compare details of silver patterns not immediately in front of him, or could remember something of little consequence she had mentioned the first time they met. What, she wondered, had he catalogued about *her* in that remarkable mind of his? Unthinkingly she moved her hands to smooth the wrinkles in her shirt.

Martin pointed to a milk jug decorated with a clear, bright blue pastoral scene. "That's a fine old Spode pitcher. Josiah Spode perfected the process of blue printing on earthenware from hand-engraved copper plates and put English potters first in the world."

"Do you know *everything*?" She shook her head in amazement.

"Hardly, but I had an inspiring teacher." When he repeated her own words, Sandy's imagination was filled with images of the wealthy, sophisticated women he had undoubtedly escorted to art auctions and parties in elegant mansions—perhaps their own—filled with similar treasures. Undoubtedly they had taught him a thing or two.

She turned from the Spode and picked up a delicate cup and saucer of faded blue willowware. "Do you know the story of willowware?" she asked.

"If this is a test, I've just failed."

"Oh, I didn't mean it that way. But it is a charming legend. The princess fell in love with the gardener. When her father, the emperor, found out, he locked her in the tiny pagoda on the island and set a guard at the bridge. The goddess of love took pity on the lovers and turned them into birds so they could fly to each other and live happily ever after in their home in the willow tree. There are lots of willowware patterns, but they all have the elements of the story; the pagoda on an island, the willow tree, and the birds."

"It is charming. I'll never see a piece of willowware again without thinking of it . . . and the one who told me the story." He took the cup from her. "And just so you won't forget it either, I'm going to get this for you."

"Oh, Martin, thank you, I'd love it."

The shop was run by a frail old woman in a black dress with a bit of lace at the collar and cuffs. Her iron-gray hair was pulled back in a tight little knot, accentuating the parchment transparency of her wrinkled skin and birdlike features. Sandy and Martin stood smiling patiently as the gnarled old hands slowly and laboriously wrote the receipt: "Genuine antique, guaranteed to be over one hundred years old."

"There now, dear," she chirped, handing the white box tied with string to Sandy, "you won't have to pay customs duty on it."

They thanked her and left the shop. "You know," laughed Martin leaning close to Sandy,

"I think the proprietress herself was the most thoroughly authentic antique in the shop."

No matter how often Sandy admonished herself, she was trembling with excitement as she dressed for dinner that night. Since she had been doing much of her sightseeing with her friends, her budget was stretching farther than she had dared hope it would, so she had allowed herself the extravagance of a new dress on her expedition to Harrod's earlier that week—primrose yellow in the soft, flowing lines she loved. When every shining lock of hair was brushed into place and her lips accented with a blush of honey almond lipstick, she surveyed herself in the looking glass. Her reflection mirrored her delight in the way the dress flattered the curves of her body and discreetly revealed her slender figure.

And when Martin called for her a few minutes later, it was evident that the effect was not lost on him.

They drove a few miles from Winchester where, on the crest of a tree-shaded hill just outside a small hamlet, Martin pulled the Rolls to a stop before a flint-and-brick wall. He held the gate open for her, then guided her through the lawn and garden to the door of an ancient cottage-type inn.

"This looks more like a private home than a public restaurant," Sandy said.

"I thought it would be your kind of place. It has centuries of history behind it."

Seated at a massive refectory table, worn smooth by long use, Sandy felt the centuries drop away. She would not have been the least bit surprised had knights in armor suddenly appeared at the gate, demanding stabling for their steeds and food and lodging for themselves and their squires.

Martin was studying the wine list. "The beef here is excellent. How about a Burgundy to go with it?"

"Not for me, thank you, Martin."

"Oh, I forgot. You don't ever touch it, do you? Religious reasons?"

"Well, in a way. I was taught not to drink, but now I know the foundation of my faith isn't based on whether or not I drink a glass of wine. But I do believe abstinence is better social policy at the very least."

Martin nodded thoughtfully and set the wine list aside. "Actually, the water here is a better choice, anyway. There's an ancient well out back that was built for the castle. It's three hundred feet deep, and legend has it King Stephen hid his treasures there."

As if on cue, the waiter set heavy glass goblets before them. The glasses were frosted with condensation, and the water, straight from the well, was crystal clear and ice cold.

"If you wish, you are welcome to inspect the

treadwheel after dinner," the waiter suggested, pointing toward the back door of the inn. "It is twelve feet in diameter and a man and donkey have to walk nearly half a mile every time water is fetched in the barrel."

"Marvelous!" said Sandy when the waiter had withdrawn. "I already love this place."

The rare, fine-grained, roast beef and crisp Yorkshire pudding were succulent, and the accompanying conversation, light and pleasant. Martin never actually told a joke, but a gentle undercurrent of humor sparkled in his comments. She noticed that laugh lines danced at the corners of his eyes when he was relaxed. Now he looked at her in that special way, and she suddenly realized she had let her heart show in her eyes. She blinked and looked away. Had he seen? Would he laugh at the silly little American who had fallen so easily under his spell? She simply *had* to build some defenses she told herself sternly. But how?

When they were finishing the last bits of the tangy, crumbly cheddar cheese with their coffee, Martin reached across the table and took her hand. "I'm glad you let me talk you into coming. I do enjoy your company."

"It's been wonderful," Sandy agreed, "and we still have another day."

"Oh, Sandra." He pulled his hand back, his face suddenly somber. "I'm afraid not. I have— ah—an engagement early tomorrow afternoon.

We'll have to get right back to London in the morning."

The joyous moment shattered like a glass and lay in jagged shards near her heart. Whatever Martin's enigmatic silence concealed, it was now between them like a living presence.

Sandy swallowed her disappointment and smiled bravely, hoping her lips weren't trembling. *Defenses*, she reminded herself. "Well, then we'd better get back to the hotel if we're to make an early start."

But Martin didn't hurry back to Winchester. Instead he turned the car east, rolled back the sun roof, switched on the radio, and drove slowly through the warm summer night.

"I thought you should see the chalk downs by moonlight," he said.

Sandy tried to blot tomorrow's "ah—engagement" out of her mind as Martin apparently had. She settled back in the cushioned seat and was suddenly aware that the radio was playing "Yankee Doodle."

"The BBC salutes the States on their birthday," came the announcer's voice.

"How charming that they would play 'Yankee Doodle' on the Fourth of July."

Martin laughed, "Just to show there are no hard feelings."

"Over the 'family quarrel'?" Sandy laughed. "I don't think most Americans are aware of how much we owe to our British heritage—our ideas of government, our legal system, our language and literature, even much of our religion. . . .''

Martin slipped his arm around her shoulder and held her tightly.

She looked straight ahead and continued. ''As an American, I feel Elizabeth I, Shakespeare, and John Wesley are just as much mine as yours, in the same way that Abraham, Moses, and David belong to me as a Christian, just as much as to my Jewish neighbors.''

''You don't know how glad I am that you feel that way, Sandra.'' Martin pulled her closer to him. She dared not look up at him, but she nestled slightly in the warmth of his embrace. Thoughts of defenses drifted away with the moonlight.

They drove on through the gentle night, Martin holding her, soft music floating from the radio.

The Sussex Downs were an enchanting surprise to Sandy, who had pictured all of England, except the Yorkshire moors, to be wooded. Before her lay a long range of chalk hills, almost devoid of features as the moon highlighted their smooth, rolling surfaces. And every crest of the road revealed a glimpse of the sea, shimmering silvery in the distance.

''Would you like to get out and walk a bit?'' Martin suggested as he stopped the car. She nodded.

They left the car and found a narrow country lane that moved gently across the rolling land.

Martin took her hand, and his warm touch became part of the magic scene, as did his rich voice: "Have you ever thought of staying longer? Living here?"

She tried to answer in a normal voice, to keep out the catch of longing. "I've thought."

"And?"

"An English teacher's moving to England— isn't that what you'd call sending coals to Newcastle?"

Martin didn't reply, and they moved on in the gentle silence of the night, broken when Sandy at last voiced her thoughts. "You can't imagine how many people told me I would be disappointed, that England wouldn't be what I'd imagined."

"And what did you imagine?"

"Well, actually I put it down in a sort of poem—if I can remember it. . . ." She knew she remembered it very well, but as so many times before, she shied at sharing anything so revealingly personal. But then their steps rounded the crest of a gentle hill and she caught a glimpse of the silver sea ringing their spellbound moment, and her words came out as soft as the air around them:

A garden and a pot of tea,
A thatched cottage with a climbing rose,
A stately country house in a green, green field,
The pomp and circumstance of kings,

The peace of a country village,
The excellence of Shakespeare and fine bone china,
The pleasure of Jane Austen and scones
     with clotted cream,
The courage of Churchill and Dunkirk,
As old as King Arthur; as new as the
     latest rock group.

"Oh, dear, I'm glad it's dark." She put her hands to her hot cheeks. "I rarely share my poetry with others."

But Martin didn't join her derision; he seemed to be thinking very seriously. "Sandra . . ." he began. That was the second time he'd done that, and again she wondered how the sentence was being completed in his mind. But she didn't find out. Instead, he took her hand and they moved on—Martin walking; Sandy, floating—in the quiet of the night, down a little curving country lane across the Downs.

But alone in her hotel room later, Sandy made a crash landing. She was frightened by how much of herself she had revealed to Martin—how close she had let him come to her heart. She was so confused, as if she were standing in the center of a mine field and had no way of knowing which inevitable step would bring the explosion. Being with Martin was wonderful, but how could she trust him? Even if he were sincere about caring for her—at the moment—what was there to prevent his deciding he liked someone better next month? Or next week? Or even tomorrow?

The explosion could come at the far end of the field, partway across, or with her next step. But that it *would* come was a foregone conclusion. After all, Brad had been a nice, steady seminary student; Martin, a playboy from the first.

She thought for a moment about the comparison. No, she insisted for the hundredth time, she wasn't bitter about Brad, but she had no intention of having to learn that lesson again. She was perfectly willing to make a new mistake, but relying on a man to fill the loneliness inside her, planning on his being there to provide the companionship she'd always longed for, allowing her feelings for him to go beyond friendship into the deeper. more fragile emotions—no, thank you. Once was quite enough.

She would stay safely, if uncomfortably, in the center of the field, and Mr. Martin Graham could stay at the edge. After all, it worked both ways; if she couldn't get across, neither could anyone get to her.


The Sunday morning trip back to London was accomplished with dispatch along the practically deserted motorway. Last night's clear sky was now overcast with clouds and threatened rain. "Our famous English weather," Martin remarked wryly.

Several times Sandy glanced at him and was startled to see a look of weighty concern, at odds with the playboy image he normally projected.

She hated to see pain in those eyes. She was reminded of his troubled look over that phone call in Cambridge. If he would talk to her about it, perhaps she could help—or at least understand. But mine fields were not proper ground for deep concerns. He would just have to remain a mystery.

Martin glanced at his watch as he set her overnight bag down outside her hotel-room door, "Just time to make it. I'll call you. Thanks for a wonderful weekend."

"Thank you, Martin." And he was gone, his long legs carrying him down the hall in a few strides.

Inside, the room looked more desolate than ever, reflecting Sandy's mood. Then she saw the white rectangle on her dresser. A letter. It must have come while she was gone and been brought up by the maid. Her eyes got misty just at the sight of the stars and stripes on the stamp. For all her love of England, her feelings for America ran just as deep—after all, loving your grandmother didn't mean you loved your mother less.

She pulled her eyes from the stamp to the address. The sight of Pam's handwriting struck her like a physical blow, bringing back in full force all the emotions she had so long suppressed and denied.

Holding the letter as if it were a snake, she carried it to her bed and sat down to think. Okay, she would admit it. She was jealous—jealous and angry and bitter. No matter how unacceptable such feelings were for a Christian, they were hers. And now, at a distance, she could admit that they had been there all the time: While she was seeing her roommate off on dates—with the man *she* loved; while she was helping Pam address wedding invitations—invitations bearing the wrong bride's name; while she was walking down the aisle as a bridesmaid—with Brad standing at the altar, waiting for someone else. And, the greatest irony of all, while she was catching the bridal bouquet!

All the time, those sour emotions were eating away, getting fat while her heart got thinner and thinner.

But to admit to them meant that she had to deal with them, just as any malignancy must be dealt with before it choked the life from its victim. *O, Lord, help me! I don't want to be like this inside. Please forgive me. Take away the ugliness and hatred and make room for Your beauty and love.*

The tension drained from her. She felt that if the atmosphere around her heart could be photographed, the pictures would show a clear progression from cold, tight, icy blues to warm, free, pulsing pinks; from darkness, emptiness, and despair to light, fullness, and joy.

A smile of peace and unhindered happiness lit her face. *"O thank You, Lord, I had no idea . . . Thank You!"* Now she could read Pam's letter.

She tore it open and flung herself on the bed to read. Pam's letter was full of excitement, describing in detail the beauties of the white Bermuda beaches and aquamarine water where they honeymooned. "And Brad has accepted a call to a church in Florida, so we'll stay with his folks in Boston for about ten days while we pack our things and then be on our way to our first home.

"Sandy, I just wish I could tell you how happy I am. It's so beautiful—sharing our spiritual relationship as well as the physical. The oneness we feel while praying together is as wonderful as the oneness we feel during the most intimate moments of our marriage.

"I'm convinced that a truly Christian marriage is the closest relationship on earth. After all, the closer two objects are to a central point, the closer they are to each other."

The letter continued, but Sandy couldn't concentrate. She now saw with absolute certainty how right Pam and Brad were for each other. The revelation was startling: Brad wasn't the one intended for her by God, but what if she and Brad *had* married? The release was like a fresh sea breeze blowing through her mind. "Thank You; thank You; thank You," she said over and over again and then laughed aloud.

She grabbed her pen and stationery to tell Pam how truly happy she was for her. But after the first line, words wouldn't come and her pen hung in midair. She thought of Martin Graham and the strange fascination he held for her . . .

The words of Pam's letter swam before her eyes; " . . . sharing our spiritual relationship as well as our physical . . . a truly Christian marriage is the closest relationship on earth . . ." That was what Sandy desired with her whole heart, but she could never have that complete unity with Martin. Their relationship would be physical only.

*How could you?* she berated herself. *How could you possibly fall in love with a man who doesn't share your faith?* She curled her hand into a tight fist and pounded the table. And now that the emotional land mines of hurt and bitterness had been defused, what would protect her from Martin?

## CHAPTER 7

THE DAYS SPED BY QUICKLY. London and its environs offered infinite sightseeing possibilities: A play in the West End, a visit to the Wellington Museum, an afternoon walk along the Embankment, and one entire day in the British Museum. It was that evening, when Sandy was lounging in her room resting her tourist-weary feet, that there was a knock on her door.

"Telephone, Miss Hollis."

Slipping her feet into sandals, she went quickly to the phone, both hoping and fearing that it would be Martin.

"Hello."

"Hullo, Sandra."

At the sound of his voice the room spun crazily and her heart thudded. "Hi, Martin." She forced herself to sound casual. With a deep breath the room righted itself—almost.

"Sorry it took me so long to get back to you, but I've been tied up."

"That's all right. I've been quite busy myself." She could never let him guess that the words, *Telephone, Miss Hollis,* and the rich, mellow sound of his voice coming through the receiver had hardly been out of her dreams day or night—especially at night when she felt the loneliness of her four walls enclosing her.

They chatted briefly about her activities, and then he said, "I want to be sure you keep Monday and Tuesday open. We'll go to Glastonbury."

"Oh, well . . ." she faltered. Why did she thrill so to the idea when she knew she was just prolonging the agony, irritating the wound so that it might never heal?

"Great!" He assumed her acceptance of his invitation. "I could hardly take you to see the Round Table without finishing the story, could I? What kind of tourist service would you think we were running over here? Matter of national pride and all that."

"But, Martin. . . ."

"Same terms as last time." She could sense the mild ridicule in his voice. He seemed to tolerate her "fanaticism," probably because he expected to break down her resistance. The idea left her too weak to protest as Martin dictated time and place for Monday morning and rang off. *He obviously views me as a challenge,* she thought miserably.

Her feet took her to her room from force of habit, but her brain was numb with the insight she'd just gained. Perhaps she was the first woman who had ever played hard-to-get with Martin, and he was amused—especially since her moral stance was a religious conviction. It was like pitting himself against God. "Oh, that abominable male ego!" She slammed her door.

All right, now the gauntlet was flung. She'd go with him, but she would not provide an ego trip for him. If she were to do battle properly, she had to be equipped, so she prepared carefully. The afternoon before the appointed zero hour she packed carefully, manicured her nails in a delicate shade of mauve pink pearl and planned a new hair style caught back on one side with a tortoise shell comb.

With the externals out of the way, she picked up her Bible to prepare the inner woman. "Finally then," she read, "find your strength in the Lord, in his mighty power. Put on all the armour which God provides . . . then you will be able to stand your ground when things are at their worst . . . Fasten on the belt of truth; for coat of mail put on integrity; . . . and, with all these, take up the great shield of faith . . ."

When her summons came the next morning, announcing Martin's presence in the lobby, she marched forth, repeating to herself, *For God and St. George!*

Taking her cases, he gave her a cheery "Good morning," and followed her from the hotel to put the cases in the boot of the Rolls. After holding the passenger door for her, he went around and slid into his own seat. "And so to Bath!" he announced. In all this time, Sandy had offered only the mildest of greetings.

Turning the car west toward the Bath road, Martin drove in silence for a time, concentrating on the heavy morning traffic. As they left the environs of the city he gave his companion a curious sidelong look. "Hmmm, cool this morning, isn't it?" he commented with a rather smug smile. Since the July sun was bright in the sky, she knew he meant the emotional temperature inside the car.

She shrugged, wishing desperately she could think of a sharp retort—a real setdown like the heroines in Regency romance novels always delivered. But nothing sufficiently clever or caustic came to mind. *I'm not very good at this,* she admitted to herself.

"Since you haven't asked about our plans for the day I can only assume, as your much-admired Jane would say, that you are simply too curious for words; so I shall attempt to enlighten you. Can those of you in the rear of the bus hear me properly?" Martin assumed the slick tones of a professional tour guide and held an imaginary

101

microphone to his mouth. "You will notice that our driver has left the main highway for this quieter, more picturesque route. Ladies and gentlemen, we are now following a road as old as the Roman occupation of Britain."

Sandy couldn't resist turning to gaze at the old leafy highway. "Appropriate oohs and aahs may now be heard from the passengers," Martin prompted. When Sandy maintained her silence, a brief smile crinkled the corners of his eyes, and he went on, unruffled, "Whether Bath was founded by the Romans or by the pigs is a moot question. But for the sake of romance, I personally favor the pigs.

"According to this picturesque, if somewhat doubtful history, the honor of founding Bath is accorded to Prince Bladud, the father of King Lear. The unhappy prince contracted the dread disease of leprosy and, amid the tears of his distraught parents and the mourning of the courtiers, suffered banishment from his father's court."

Martin tapped his imaginary microphone on the steering wheel and blew into it, "Is this thing working? Anyone who cannot hear me, please raise your hand . . . in the back of the bus?" He looked toward Sandy. She nodded, really wanting to hear the rest of the story. "Very well, in acquiescence to the overwhelming response of its patrons, we continue our narrative.

"The wretched prince obtained work as a

102

swineherd and forthwith contaminated the herd. Alarmed by this development, and fearful of returning to his master, he drove his herd across the river Avon. From this place, still called Swineford, he ascended the surrounding hills— in the hollows of which sprang secret springs. The swine soon discovered the water and proceeded to indulge their love of muck. It took the distracted prince considerable time to dislodge the porkers from their quagmire, but when, that evening, he came to wash them down, he discovered they were rid of their leprosy.

"Thinking two and two just might make four, the prince himself decided to wallow. He emerged, like Naaman after his seventh dip in the muddy Jordan, cured of leprosy. Upon driving his pigs back to his master, he procured his release and set forth for his father's court where he was received with great joy. And in tribute to the place that brought about his cure, he founded a royal city, where he reigned happily for many years."

Sandy was fascinated by the story, but remained silent, her armor intact. The more skillfully Martin attempted to draw her out, the more she became convinced that it was a ploy—a ploy for winning the game, with herself as the prize.

"Tips are not necessary," he concluded his clever spiel, "but applause is appreciated and all fan mail will be answered personally." Sandy looked at him, smiling briefly, though disgusted with herself for enjoying what was so obviously a manipulative device. "Sandra, what's gotten into you? You've hardly spoken to me. What is the matter?"

"Nothing's the matter. I'm just not in a very talkative mood." She moved one shoulder in a halfhearted shrug.

"Very well," he nodded with a note of finality and they continued in silence until the road ended in all the splendor of Bath, set in her crescent of hills.

They crossed Pulteney Bridge, a covered arcade of shops that spanned the river Avon, and drew to a stop at a nearby car park. A short walk brought them to a small town square where they paused before an aged statue.

"Look!" Sandy cried, forgetting her pique with Martin. "It's King Bladud!" At the base of the statue, a plaque was inscribed with the words: "'The eighth king of the Britons, descended from Brute, a great philosopher and mathematician bred at Athens, and founder of the baths in 863 B.C.'" She smiled. "Well then, that settles it—the pigs won!" It was all too magical for Sandy to maintain her frosty façade. No sense letting her desire to teach Martin a lesson ruin her day. She could at least put up the visor on her helmet.

"It certainly was settled in the minds of the inhabitants of Bath in 1699, at least," agreed Martin, reading the plaque over her shoulder. He refrained from commenting on her sudden thaw and made no attempt to draw her closer to him.

After lunch, a meal which always left Sandy longing for a crisp, fresh American salad such as she had failed to encounter on this side of the Atlantic, they viewed the ancient Roman baths behind the Cathedral and watched the progress of an archeological dig in one of the baths.

The afternoon passed pleasantly—outwardly, at least. But inside, Sandy was in a turmoil of doubt and vacillation. She didn't want Martin to touch her; she did want him to take her in his arms. She wanted to give him a sharp, stinging setdown; she wanted to make him smile and laugh and enjoy her company. She wanted never to see him again; she wanted to be with him always.

She thought of the past weeks, how God had obviously been leading her one step at a time, how He had brought her to a clear understanding of and freedom from her past hurts. But what was the next step? Her plan that morning, to keep some emotional distance from Martin, had obviously been unsuccessful. Perhaps the next step should be to relax and allow a real friendship to develop with Martin.

Just the idea was relaxing. It would be so much easier— but *only* a friendship—that was the rub.

Leaving Bath behind them, they drove through a tiny village, all of stone, timber, and thatch, looking as if it had dropped from the pages of a storybook. "How old are these places?" she asked.

"Some are ancient; others go no further back than Queen Anne's time," he replied.

Sandy laughed, "Queen Anne? Early 1700's— or was it late 1600's? And you speak of it as if it were only yesterday. What a long perspective you English have."

"Well, isn't that what history does—helps you put your own life and time in perspective?"

Martin swung again into his tour guide narrative. "And now, ladies and gentlemen, to the right of the bus you will note an inn built of the attractive ruddy stone of this region, with a pantiled roof. I wish to draw your attention to the characteristic west country style of the cylindrical chimney . . ."

With fairy-tale enchantment, Sandy gazed at the warm red sandstone building, its round chimney clinging to the surface of the wall and rising on up like a mighty tree trunk. Martin went on to describe the stone bridge, which had been built for medieval pack ponies, keeping the sides low so as not to disturb their packs.

"Oh, Martin, I love it all so much!" Sandy at last gave free voice to the feelings she had kept bottled up all morning.

"Better than applause; the management thanks you." And the management's thanks was expressed with his very special smile.

Sandy rolled down her window. Hay scented

the air and when the car slowed down for an ancient farm truck ahead of them, the call of a wood pigeon sounded peacefully above the hum of road noises. The Rolls traveled smoothly through the Mendip Hills, and for awhile all that existed for Sandy was sun and air and speed, only the green fields and the shadows of the clouds that fled across them, the whispering beechtree woods, the sun-flecked meadows, and the round green hills reaching to the sky.

They achieved the crest of the last hill and suddenly before Sandy spread a vision of pinnacled stone towers rising above rounded masses of green foliage.

"Wells," Martin said. He parked the car and they walked slowly toward the great building before them.

"One side trip before the cathedral," Martin explained, turning up a tiny street to their right, and picked up his narrative. "Vicar's Close— reputed to be the most complete ancient street in Europe. Built in the fourteenth century, the street and its uniform stone houses, which you see before you, ladies and gentlemen, belong to the vicars of the cathedral. It remains substantially as it has been for six hundred years."

Sandy laughed. "Did you memorize the whole guidebook?"

"The Graham Tour Service offers nothing but the best," he replied.

Sandy was enchanted by the row of houses

with their tall chimneys and beautifully tended gardens. The little lawns spilled a profusion of scented flowers—roses, fuchsia, hydrangea, and lavender.

At the end of the street they turned and made their way back toward the cathedral and, as she had so many times in the past weeks, Sandy felt herself transported back in time. But for their modern clothes and the cars in the street, they could easily have stepped through a time door into medieval England.

"I'm taking you in the back way for my favorite view of the cathedral," Martin explained as they crossed the street and entered the close.

The cathedral, springing from the azure depths of crystalline pools, from emerald lawns, and surrounded by arching trees—making homes for cawing rooks and soaring pigeons—was a thrilling sight. Sandy stood dwarfed and speechless beside it.

"A church has stood near this site since King Ina of the West Saxons founded one about A.D. 700. The cathedral has stood very much as you see it today for almost five hundred years." Martin's words were professional tour guide quality, but the intensity of tone with which they were spoken betrayed a deep feeling for the scene before him.

Sandy jumped at the sound of chimes from the three gray, timeworn towers above her head. The music of the bells vibrated on the air and then died away.

" 'Lord, through this hour, be Thou our guide; That by Thy power, No foot may slide'," Martin quoted the words of the music.

Sandy's heart raced. If he really meant those words, maybe there was hope. But no, she counseled herself, it's just religion to him—a tradition and an ethic—not a vital personal experience. Not an experience to be shared as Pam and Brad shared their life. She turned sadly away.

"Where are the swans?" she asked, when she had conquered the burning lump in her throat. "Do they really ring a bell when they are hungry?"

"Indeed they do. This way, if you please, milady." Their walk took them beside the natural spring at the back of the cathedral—the seven wells from which the city took its name. The water surged up in a dome from the unfathomed depths of a translucent pool. They walked along a narrow walkway that followed the brook, bounding in an impetuous cascade to the moat around the Bishop's Palace. There the water rested in glassy stillness over branching, feathery, starlike water weeds.

Sandy gasped, "A real moat!"

"Yes, a real moat with a real drawbridge. Unfortunately, the drawbridge is up today—no visitors allowed."

And then they came gliding by—serene, stately, pristine white—the proud inhabitants of the moat. "Surely, those aren't swans. They're spellbound princes, living among the lilies of the moat . . ."

"And waiting to be kissed to life by a beautiful maiden?" Martin finished for her. He bent down swiftly and kissed her. A brief kiss but one that left her lips tingling.

*He thinks he can do that anytime the mood strikes him, I'll bet,* she thought angrily, more furious with herself because of the weakness in her knees than with Martin for having caused it. *Only friendship,* she reminded herself.

"Why?" she asked, looking again at the swans.

"Well, because I had rather hoped you'd like it," he said, frowning.

Sandy couldn't control a helpless burst of laughter. "Oh, no, no! I didn't mean *why the kiss!* I meant why do the swans ring bells to eat?"

And again the impersonal tour guide appeared. "No one knows for sure, but it is believed that a daughter of a bishop in Victorian days trained them. It seems the young lady had time on her hands and with infinite patience contrived to impress on contemporary swan intellects, such as they were, that if they took hold of the cord that hung a few feet above the water from a window in the gate tower, and gave it a sharp yank with their beaks, something went ting-a-ling and manna dropped from heaven.

"Not these swans, of course, but their ancestors, and the knowledge has been handed down through generations of swans. Now, ladies and gentlemen, if any of you have a bit of scone in your pocket left over from tea, you may respond, should your services be requested."

Sandy laughed at his act; he was really very good. She found herself deeply regretting, even more than the barrier between them, the *necessity* for the barrier. *If only* . . . . she sighed. The swans didn't seem to be ready to take tea, because no bells jingled.

"Speaking of tea," said Martin, "it's past time. We can come back and do the interior later. All right with you?"

"Of course," Sandy agreed, realizing suddenly that she was hungry.

They walked along an avenue of stately elms to the sign of the Swan above a narrow street. The smiling, white-aproned maid brought a silver tea tray, laden with hot toast, cakes, and scalding, heavenly tea, to their table by the window.

"I will put a bit of scone in my pocket, just in case I should encounter a hungry swan," Sandy said, as she lifted one of the steaming fresh biscuits from the white linen folds of its basket and spread it generously with butter.

Refreshed by the stop, they made their way back to the cathedral grounds, back to the close and cloister, through the carved stone gateway called Penniless Porch where beggars of yesteryear had congregated, past the brilliant gardens and across the clipped green lawn, to the flowing waters and timeless elms. They approached slowly, almost humbly, across the green, while the beauty of the façade grew before their eyes. At last they stood, very small, on the graveled path that ran along the front.

"It's so . . . so . . . still," Sandy whispered with a glory-stricken catch of her breath. "Peaceful. Serene," she uttered, not moving her eyes from row after row of stone figures clad in medieval costumes.

"Sleeping Beauty?" Martin suggested.

"Yes, that's it. Enchanted . . . like the silence after music has stopped, but still lingers on the air."

They entered the arched doorway beneath the tier upon tier of more than four hundred statues. Inside the lonely nave, the fading sunlight shone through the western window, casting its color on sculptured tombs and carved ornaments and on gray stone walls. For the first time that day, Martin took her hand, and Sandy did not resist.

Inside the cathedral Sandy felt even greater tranquility. With the murmur of prayer and praise stilled, it seemed as if the worship of the devout who had knelt here through the ages was still present. As they stood looking at the double rows of gothic arches lining the nave, the organ began to play, pulsating its notes through the stony frame. And then the great solemn place was filled with the thrilling sweetness of boyish voices joining the deeper voice of the organ. It was a moment transfixed in time and Sandy's heart joined in their tuneful, long amen as it rang and resounded down the empty nave and echoed again and again from distant chapel and far-receding vaults.

Without a word they turned slowly and walked into the English dusk. But Sandy felt that a bit of her soul remained behind in that magnificent cathedral to intercede for the future. The future that she must face alone when the bubble burst and Cinderella returned to her hearth. Well, she supposed that grading papers beat sweeping ashes.

Martin had made reservations for them at the George and Pilgrims Inn in Glastonbury just five miles away, a grand stone building that looked as if it would have been at home within the cathedral enclosure.

"Tradition holds that during the dissolution, Henry VIII stayed here and watched the burning of the Abbey from that window," Martin pointed.

"Like Nero watching Rome burn," Sandy shuddered. But the welcoming inn held no ghosts for her.

Sandy dressed for dinner with some apprehension. Even her red silk did not provide the reassurance she needed to face the evening ahead. When she was alone she could think clearly and decisively as to where her relationship with Martin must stop. But when she was with him. . . . She sighed and shook her head, "You're really hopeless," she told her mirrored image.

Martin was using the lobby phone when she came down the stairs. She sank into one of the overstuffed chairs to wait for him, idly scanning the magnificent oak paneling and the fireplace of old blue and white tiles. But her eyes kept straying to the well-shaped head that was bent slightly forward as Martin talked into the receiver. His dark brown sport jacket of a nubby weave hung so perfectly from his broad shoulders that it must have been tailor-made, she thought.

As she watched, the shoulders slumped as if in defeat, and he replaced the receiver slowly before turning to her. Sandy caught her breath at the grim look on his face, revealing deep lines of frustration or anxiety that she had never seen there before. Her first impulse was to reach out and smooth away those lines, but that would be stepping beyond the bounds of simple friendship.

"You look like Atlas bearing the weight of the world." And then she did hold out her hand to him.

He grasped her outstretched hand and sank into a chair beside her. "Not quite that, I hope. Just of England."

"Another emergency?" And as she spoke, she realized the change in her attitude—that she now believed in his emergencies as something more than a playboy's excuse.

He nodded, "I have to go to Yorkshire."

"Tonight?"

"No. I simply told them that was out of the question. But early tomorrow. Listen, Sandra, the abbey is within shouting distance. You really must see it. We'll run by in the morning, though the holiest earth in all of England shouldn't be rushed over. But then—" he paused uneasily, "would you mind terribly going north with me? It'll be much faster if I go straight up through Birmingham rather than back through London, and it will give you a chance to see that part of the country. I am sorry, Sandra."

The disappointments of her earlier years had taught Sandy to take it on the chin—no matter how many years she had spent daydreaming of leisurely hours at Glastonbury and maybe even going on down to Tintagel, the rugged castle by the sea where legend placed Arthur's birth. And she had learned years ago that making a fuss could only make a bad situation worse. Whatever Martin thought of her, there was no reason to add "poor sport" to the list.

"Sure," she shrugged with a smile. "Why not?"

## CHAPTER 8

GLASTONBURY. Here was Arthur's Isle of Avalon. Here, Joseph of Arimathea came with a band of disciples, bearing the holy grail. Here, St. Patrick organized the scattered hermits of Avalon into a semblance of order. Here, Arthur and Guinevere lay in a single grave. Here was founded the first Christian church in Britain. Here, for a thousand years, was the ground held in such veneration that the great from all over Europe were brought for burial. How many books Sandy had pored over, memorizing every detail. How long she had dreamed of walking on this sacred turf. Now she was here.

The exquisite broken arches cast long shadows on the green lawn in the early morning sunlight as Sandy and Martin slipped through the turnstile and made their way to the remains of the ruined abbey. They were quite alone. No other tourists had ventured out so early.

"The *size* of it," breathed Sandy. "The peace and dignity of it." Wordlessly, Martin slipped his arm around her and stood sharing the immensity of the moment.

"The fragments have outlived the blasphemy done to them. They have been redeemed again to holiness and beauty," he said softly.

Her heart leaped. "Martin, that's beautiful. You've captured my feeling exactly." With an aching throat Sandy moved ahead of him down the sun-flecked nave toward the high altar.

At length, she turned back toward him and spoke again, "Do you believe it?"

"Believe what?" he asked.

"About the excavated tomb? I want to believe that Lancelot brought the body of the repentant Guinevere here from her nunnery to lie at the feet of the husband they had wronged. But is it childish? Like believing in Santa Claus?"

"It is perfectly credible and also perfectly unprovable. But when I stand here, I believe it."

"Yes, there's something about it . . . there's no other place exactly like it. Even if I hadn't come here knowing this was the holiest ground in England, I'm sure I would have sensed it." Sandy felt Martin's arm around her waist again. She appreciated his companionship, his closeness. They were sharing a profound moment— touching the roots of their race and their church.

"I am so sorry, Sandra. It's a sacrilege to rush this," Martin said as he led her back to the car. But she really didn't mind. She had experienced Glastonbury. Anything more could only be anti-climactic.

They turned their backs on the abbey, leaving the unroofed and dishonored chapel, the fragment of aisle wall, the crumbling stones of the choir, and the two titan piers of the chancel arch. Slipping into the front seat, Sandy raised her eyes to bid farewell to Glastonbury Tor and the low and softly rounded hills surrounding it.

They drove through dips in the low-lying hills, across swelling downs and pastures and beside flowery gardens. A softer, sweeter country one could not call up in dreams—rich and fertile, breathed over by soft winds and smiled upon by a gentle summer morning sun. "As if God's finger touched, but did not press in making England," Sandy murmured.

"What?"

"Elizabeth Barrett Browning—I was quoting again."

Martin nodded in reply, but it was easy to see that his mind was not on poetry, nor on the gentle beauty of the countryside. His expression was anxious and weary, his manner tense, as the Rolls ate up the miles northward. The names on turn-off roads read like the pages of a guidebook: Stratford-on-Avon, Warwick, Coventry. But the silver car bore steadily on its course. To Sandy's left rose the green heights of the Peak District of the Pennines—the mountains she had noticed on the map running like a backbone down the center of the land.

Her eyes roamed the rocky outcroppings on the high verdant moorland, and once or twice she caught sight of parties of hikers or picnickers in the grassy landscape. The thought crossed her mind that it would be fun to share a picnic tea with Martin on the sun-warmed slopes, but as she glanced at his profile, looking more foreboding than the rocky landscape, she knew the holiday spirit was over. For whatever reason, it was over.

Sandy realized she was hurt that Martin shut her out so completely—as if he had forgotten her. And yet, as she surreptitiously studied his handsome features, she felt a wrench of compassion for the troubled man she saw. The mirth in his eyes was extinguished; the laugh lines weren't dancing now. She was overwhelmed by a desire to help him, to share the heavy burden he was shouldering. If only he would confide in her.

It was the traditional stiff upper lip that had seen this country through Dunkirk, the Battle of Britain, and more recent economic disasters. Sandy admired it, but at the same time wanted to break through it. She longed to reach out to him, to ease the load, to relieve the turmoil. Her own unhappiness didn't matter; she would deal with that later. Right now his struggle was her own.

But how could she help him when he didn't even know she was there?

*Show me what to do,* she prayed.

They drove through the bustling city of York, past the stupendous York Minster with its arches, towers, and spires dwarfing the city and everything else around it. With York behind them they turned northwesterly, following the river Ouse.

At the end of a long avenue of linden trees and midway around a sweeping circle drive, the Rolls halted in front of a great Palladian country house—one that could easily have been ripped from the pages of a book on the great homes of Britain. "Well, here we are."

Sandra started at the sound of his voice. It must have been an hour since he had last spoken to her. Two dark-suited footmen hurried down broad front stairs. One opened Sandy's door and offered his hand to help her out; the other began receiving Martin's instructions regarding their luggage. Martin led her up the stairs.

"This is Miss Hollis, Thomas. She will be staying a few days. Show her to a room."

"Very good, sir."

And saying something to the dazed Sandy about seeing her at dinner, Martin turned abruptly and strode across the polished parquet floor to disappear through massive double doors on the far side.

"This way, if you please, Miss." Sandy turned

at the sound of the butler's words. The little procession, Thomas first, Sandy following, the footman bearing her bags trailing to the rear, ascended the broad curving staircase. Along the balustraded balcony they went, up another flight of stairs, down a long paneled hall, through an oak door, coming to a stop in a suite of rooms Sandy could hardly have imagined to exist anywhere outside Buckingham Palace itself.

"Your sitting room, Miss Hollis," Thomas said, indicating the room before them. Sandy blinked, looking at the carpet and draperies in a rich floral pattern and the baroque gilt furniture upholstered in rose and ivory. She wanted to run to the bay window at the far side of the room and survey the gardens below, but she supposed well-bred English ladies observed a little more restraint in front of the servants.

Thomas opened double doors to the left and introduced Sandy to her bedroom. A tapestry was spread on the enormous four-poster bed; and chairs, chaise, and pillows reflected colors of gold and rose in lace-trimmed satin and velvet.

"Dressing room and bath this way, Miss," and Thomas led her through a mirror-lined dressing room to a bathroom that looked as if it had been carved out of a single block of roseate marble. The ornate gold fixtures and thick ruby towels were its only ornamentation.

Thomas led the way back to the sitting room and gave a peremptory tug on the needlepoint bell pull hanging beside the fireplace. Almost immediately the door to the sitting room opened and a girl about Sandy's own age hurried in. "This is Miss Hollis, Barton. She is to be our guest for a few days. You will attend her." Before the maid could reply or Sandy could ask any questions, he had crossed to the door. There he turned and paused, "Tea will be served shortly on the terrace and dinner is at eight, Miss. Just ring if you need anything."

"Shall I unpack for you, then, Miss?" the maid asked.

"Oh . . . yes, I suppose so," Sandy turned to focus on the maid. "Yes, please do," she said in a more decided voice. People in books always refused an offer to have their bags unpacked, but Sandy thought it would be a delightful service— hardly one she was offered every day.

"Excuse my asking, but you're an American, aren't you, Miss?" Barton asked as she turned immediately to her work.

"Yes, I am. I'm just visiting England for the summer."

"I do hope you're having a good holiday."

"Yes, I certainly am. It's wonderful." Sandy smiled to herself, surveying her surroundings, and added—*full of surprises, but wonderful*.

It didn't take the girl long to unpack Sandy's two cases and arrange everything neatly— clothes hanging in the dressing room, shoes on shelves, lingerie in the chest of drawers, cosmetics on the dresser. "Will there be anything else, Miss?"

"I don't think so, thank you." The maid turned to go. "Oh, Barton, whose home is this?"

It was obvious the maid attempted to hide her surprise, but her eyes were large as she said, "Why, Lord Lindley's, Miss. It's been in his family for ever so long—since the time of William and Mary, I should think."

Sandy nodded. "Oh, I see. Well, thank you again."

The maid closed the door softly behind her and Sandy stared after her, "Thank you ever so, I'm sure," she said in a mock-British dialect. "But who is Lord Lindley?"

It was time for tea, but Sandy was unsure of the labyrinth of halls and stairs and not at all sure she would feel comfortable in the presence of Lord Lindley and his guests—even though Martin would surely be there. Instead, she walked about the beautiful suite of rooms for a bit, admiring the paintings adorning the walls: delicate watercolor studies of flowers and seascapes that might have been done by a Victorian lady, perhaps the very one who occupied these chambers; sumptuous oils in heavy gold frames, of floral bouquets and ladies wearing Georgian dresses.

She turned to the books on the shelves on either side of the white marble fireplace in her sitting room. The English teacher in her was thrilled at the collection. It spanned the whole range of English novels, from Richardson and Fielding to Dick Francis and Mary Stewart. Since she was in Yorkshire, and probably not far from Haworth and the moors, the thought of reading *Jane Eyre* again seemed immensely appealing. She hadn't read it for years and it would be fun to meet those people on their home turf. She settled on the chaise, but had read only a few pages when she found herself up and wandering around the room again.

She knelt on the rose velvet cushions of the window seat and gazed at the scene before her. Her room was on the back side of the house and the lawn spread out in three terraces below her. The first terrace was largely taken up with a formal garden of clipped boxwood in an intricate design of dark green swirls and scrolls, each section of the pattern filled with vividly colored flowers. From her vantage point, it looked like a carpet of thickly embossed velvet spread out before her. A marble balustrade ran along the clipped green grass at the edge of the terrace and was decorated with white marble statues and benches.

A stairway led to the next level, centered by a rectangular reflecting pool and bordered by banks of flowers. Then the green turf rolled down a gentle decline to the third level, surrounded by a colorful herbaceous border and a clipped hedge. Beyond the hedge spread a woods embracing meadow, lake, and streams and undoubtedly an abundance of wildlife. And there were enticing glimpses of other gardens that she must explore later. She sat spellbound for some time until a sharp pang in her stomach reminded her that she could not live on beauty alone. It was tea time and she had eaten nothing since a very early hurried breakfast of a hard roll and coffee.

She walked to the fireplace and with a sense of timelessness that could transport her to any period—Georgian, Regency, Victorian—she put her hand to the bell rope.

Somewhere in the depths of that perplexity of rooms the message was apparently delivered that Miss Hollis was in want of something, and a footman was immediately dispatched.

"I wonder if I might have some tea, please?"

"Certainly, Miss. India or China?"

"India, please, in a china pot." She smiled as she said the words. She had read that phrase somewhere and always thought it a delightful response, but had never dreamed she would have the occasion to use it. At least it seemed to impress the footman suitably. And he impressed her—she didn't know people still had footmen—except the queen, of course.

This time she settled on the gilt sofa in the sitting room to await the arrival of the tea tray. She admired the bowl of fresh flowers on the table by the sofa—roses, of course, to match the roses on carpet and drapery. They filled the room with their fragrance and Sandy couldn't wait to walk in the garden that had produced them.

A knock at the door announced the arrival of a silver tray laden with tiny sandwiches, rich little cakes, thin slices of brown bread and butter with strawberry jam, and of course the amber-brown liquid that had come to be the epitome of gracious living in Sandy's mind. The china pot was adorned with roses and a touch of gold, as was her thin china cup. A rosebud in a silver vase completed the tray.

Sandy had almost finished her last cup of tea when, in spite of the beauty around her, an intangible feeling of uneasiness began to gnaw at her. Perhaps it could be explained by fatigue and unfamiliarity with her surroundings, but a sense that something was not as it ought to be closed in on her—as if the air around her was suddenly more oppressive. She felt more totally alone than she had at any time since leaving Boston.

*Nonsense!* she told herself sharply. *It's just your hyperactive imagination because you know Yorkshire is a secluded region and . . . and . . .* she could have finished with *and because you're missing Martin,* but she simply stopped with the stern reprimand to herself and slipped between the crisp sheets of the oversized bed for a nap.

## CHAPTER 9

SHE AWOKE REFRESHED. A hot bath, and the world would be right again. She turned the gold-scrolled faucets—mixer faucets, even—and steaming water tumbled from the mouth of a golden dolphin, filling the oval, pink marble tub with luxurious bubbles. Sandy wound her hair in a loose knot on the top of her head, submerged her slim body in the frothy water and filled the huge bath sponge with hot soapy water—the soap had a lovely lavender scent—then squeezed it gently and rubbed her delicate skin. Her body tingled as the water poured over her. Finally she emerged, pink and radiant, to be enveloped in the folds of her thick ruby bath towel.

She chose her apricot voile to wear to dinner and dressed carefully. Time was such a luxury. She was leaving the room when Sandy noticed an apricot-pink rose in the bowl by the sofa that just matched her dress, so she slipped it out of the bouquet and clipped it in the soft sweep of her hair.

Finding her way down the halls and galleries to the stairway was not as difficult as she had expected. Sandy descended the great bare staircase slowly, a fitting pace for one who was walking where generations had passed before, feeling a polished smoothness from the caress of the many silk and satin skirts that had slipped from stair to stair through the centuries. She moved her hand over the wide banister, buffed to a mellow glow by numberless hands in the past. At the bottom of the wide staircase a footman waited to escort her. "I believe they are just going in to dinner now. Right this way, Miss."

Sandy was so struck by the beauty of the dining gallery she was hardly aware of the people filling it until a strong hand claimed her and she became aware of the man drawing her into the room. Martin's innate elegance was enhanced tonight by a black tuxedo with velvet collar and stiffly tucked and studded shirt. He moved easily with a grace born to such refinement.

He smiled at Sandy, turning the full perception of those heavily browed, thickly lashed eyes on her, "I've been watching for you."

"Vigilance is rewarded," she smiled back at him.

"Indeed it is. Come meet the other guests. We

missed you at tea. This is Sir Hugh Acton—"
Martin presented a plump, balding man in a
military uniform—"and Lady Hugh," a refined-
looking lady with her silver-gray hair piled
becomingly on her head.

*Lady Hugh*, thought Sandy—she'd never understand how these titles worked.

"May I present Miss Sandra Hollis, our guest
from the States." Lady Hugh gave a polite
acknowledgment, but there was no time for
conversation, for Martin was leading Sandy to
the far end of the room and, not for the first time,
she was grateful for the many hours during her
college days when she had worked in the president's home. None of those dinner parties had
risen to the splendor of this occasion, but they
had somewhat prepared her for this moment.

Martin held a chair for Sandy to the left of the
host's empty seat, and then, to her surprise, sat
at the head of the table himself. She had supposed that would be Lord Lindley's place and
had been anxious to see him. She was disappointed that he was away for the evening and was
about to say so to Martin when a slight stir at the
other end of the room caught her attention. The
men rose from their seats, signaling the arrival of
a petite raven-haired woman. It was the woman
from the airplane. She smiled charmingly at the
guests as she swept toward Martin. "Darling,
how naughty I am to be late. I am afraid I
oversleep. I see I miss the sherry hour complete-

ly." Her thickly accented voice was startlingly husky for so small a woman.

While Sandy watched woodenly, Martin kissed the delicate hand held out to him and assured the newcomer that no harm had been done, other than depriving them of her presence.

The woman was seated at Martin's right and the gentlemen resumed their seats. Martin then presented Sandy to Anya Gabrovo, then turned from Sandy and, throughout the first course of consommé royale, remained engaged in a tête-à-tête with the stunning woman of the intriguing voice. Sandy was thankful for Sir Hugh Acton's sincerely expressed concern that she enjoy her time in England.

"I can't imagine how it would be possible not to enjoy my visit here," she assured him. "It's so beautiful and everyone is helpful and friendly." The consommé was replaced with a rich, fluffy lobster mousse, which Sandy found delectable. While Martin remained engrossed with the lady to his right, Sir Hugh regaled Sandy with an account of his recent fishing expeditions to Scotland.

"But now this fall when the hunting begins. . . ." He was an excellent dinner partner for one whose mind was distracted. Sandy couldn't keep her thoughts off the woman seated across from her. Anya's shining gray dress emphasized her black eyes and lashes, which remained raised meltingly to Martin's—and showed off to perfection her smooth olive skin—a great deal of skin. Few of Anya Gabrovo's considerable charms had been left to the imagination.

The rack of lamb was accompanied by a rainbow of vegetables—nuggets of carrots, tiny red beets, snowy white cauliflower, and fresh green beans. Sandy took small portions of everything, but refused the "Potatoes Anna." The impression that the dish had been prepared in the other woman's honor was just too much for her.

" . . . and then at the very next covey the dogs gave tongue and we bagged three brace of grouse . . ." The hunting stories continued and Sandy smiled at the kindly gentleman who was doing his best to entertain her.

Romaine leaves bathed (or to Sandy's mind, drowned) in oil and vinegar were next. The exquisite chocolate mousse that followed left Sandy no appetite for the smooth, creamy, pale yellow Wensleydale cheese and fruit, which concluded the meal.

Sandy could only assume that the woman in the gold crepe gown seated at the foot of the table was Lady Lindley, as she acted the role of hostess by rising and suggesting that the ladies take their coffee in the drawing room. Sandy smiled warmly at Sir Hugh, who was helping her with her chair, and with only a brief nod to Martin, she left the room.

"I believe you're Sandra Hollis, our American visitor, am I right?" The gold-clad hostess approached Sandy. "I am Miriam Webster, Lord Lindley's aunt."

"Oh, I'm pleased to meet you. I thought perhaps you were Lady Lindley."

"No, my dear, Lord Lindley is unmarried. That's why I often do hostess duty for him. But if rumors are to be credited, I believe I may soon be relieved of the task. We shall all be very happy when Lord Lindley takes a wife."

Sandy was about to ask his lordship's whereabouts when Lady Hugh joined her, and their hostess moved on to her other guests. "I do hope my husband didn't bore you to tears with his interminable hunting and fishing tales, my dear."

"Oh, not at all. I thoroughly enjoyed him, Lady Hugh."

"You must call me Celia. Everyone does."

"Thank you. But I don't understand why your title is Lady Hugh, rather than Lady Celia?"

"Because it is my husband's title. I just married into it. If it were my own, then I would be Lady Celia. Come now, you must meet the others." Sandy was presented to the other women in the room, but found the names and titles so utterly confusing, she knew she wouldn't be able to remember any of them. "And now, we must greet our guest of honor," she continued.

Sandy took a deep breath and walked beside Lady Hugh toward Anya Gabrovo when, to their surprise, she turned abruptly from them and flew to the door of the drawing room.

"You darling men, you pretend to cherish your brandy and cigars in private, but I know you cannot stay away from us for so long." The gentlemen who were just entering through the double doors laughed appreciatively and Anya draped herself on Martin's arm. "My protectorate is doing fine job. No?" She smiled up at him. "Shall we go out for some fresh air now, darling?"

Martin removed her arm gently, but still held her hand, "I'm afraid you must excuse me, Anya. I have promised to show Miss Hollis the rose garden."

Sandy hoped she didn't look as surprised as she felt. This was certainly the first she had heard of such a promise. He stepped to her and took her arm. "Are you ready, Sandra?"

They walked a few steps from Anya before she questioned him. "*See* the rose garden in the dark?" she asked under her breath.

"Oh, it's much the best way to begin," he responded. "By daylight the color is so overwhelming one misses the other charms. In the dark you can see it with your other senses first."

To her surprise Barton met them outside the drawing room with a lacy fringed shawl, which Martin draped over her shoulders. "The efficiency here is astounding. I think the staff must be telepathic," Sandy said.

"I'm glad you find it so. You mustn't hesitate to ask for anything you want." *But what I truly want, I can never ask for, nor accept if it were offered,* she thought sadly.

Their feet crunched lightly on the white graveled paths between the rose beds, and the water of the fountain in the center of the garden splashed softly. In another part of the garden a bird sang a plaintive note, calling its lost love.

Martin guided her hand to touch the petals of a dark full-blown blossom. "It feels like velvet," she said, "only much softer, and much, much more fragile."

And as she was caressing the soft petals, Martin was stroking her cheek. "Yes, softer than velvet," he said in her ear.

"And the fragrance," she said, turning away from the danger that was Martin Graham, her feet again softly crunching on the pebbles, "I had no idea there were so many different rose scents—sweet, mild, spicy. I thought rose was rose." She felt an urge to keep on talking, to hold him at some intangible length. "It's wonderful," she continued, "like compensation for blindness. We miss so much when we rely on only the most obvious sense."

They were in the center of the garden by the fountain when he took her in his arms. "Sandra . . ." he murmured, and that one word drowned out the sound of the fountain. With one last effort her mind told her heart, *Only friendship,* and then she was lost.

The first tingle his touch had produced on the

banks of the Cam had now grown until that spark lighted her whole existence. She felt the entire garden was aglow—surely all of Yorkshire could see it—all of England.

He released her and they drew apart just enough that she could look at him. She shook her head at the wonder of being in this man's embrace in an enchanted rose garden in England. This was the stuff dreams were made of— dreams and fairy tales. The moment was pure fantasy—a culmination of every story she had ever read. She dreaded ever waking to discover that it had all been only a dream.

And then they were walking again, his arm encircling her waist, her head resting against his shoulder. A breeze caught the fragrance of roses and carried it back to her. "It was so beautiful, Martin," she said softly.

"I'll bring you again in the morning. Now you're ready for the colors."

They were nearing the house now. "I'm afraid to go in, I must look a mess."

Martin laughed gently, "I expect you couldn't if you tried. But let's not go in yet. I've hardly seen you today." He indicated a bench between two large yew trees that stood like dark sentries.

Sandy nestled her head against him and slipped her hand inside his coat to feel the beating of his heart. It made her feel very close to him . . . too close, she pulled away a fraction and made an attempt at conversation. "How's your emergency?" She had noticed earlier in the evening that the drawn look was gone and he seemed perfectly at ease.

"Under control."

*Well,* she told herself, *you should have known better than to expect an informative answer.* After a brief pause she tried again. "Martin, where is Lord Lindley? Why does he have all these guests when he's not here?"

Martin turned to her with his mouth open, then threw back his head and laughed helplessly. "My dear Sandra, didn't you know? You've just been kissing him in the rose garden!"

"What! But that doesn't make sense. Your name isn't Lindley."

"No, just my title. And has been—through about sixteen generations."

"But how is it possible I didn't know before? I mean, Karen never said anything, or . . ."

"Well, it isn't the sort of thing one puts on a hoarding— billboard to you –and I don't really use the title often. Except here, of course. It goes with the place."

Her mind was whirling. But of course it made sense—the deference shown him at Westminster, the special parking spot, "The tea room . . ." she said aloud.

"For members of Parliament only. Yes, since Dad's death I have the ancestral seat in the House of Lords and try to do my duty by it. A lot of work goes with a title if it's done properly. You don't mind, do you?"

"Mind?" *What a strange thing to ask.* "Why should I . . ."

Voices of the company floated down from the terrace and they turned with reluctance to join them. "Duty," Martin said, and in the light from the windows she could see his eyebrow, again raised at her.

"There you are, darling," Anya claimed her prey. "The rose garden was sweet?" she asked Sandy, but turned away without giving her a chance to reply.

Feeling no desire to socialize, Sandy quietly retreated to her room.

She lay in her bed, the comfort of it lost on her as she thrashed about in her mind, trying to sort it all out. Martin Graham was Lord Lindley, a peer of the realm. His kisses brought her transports of delight, and then he immediately turned back to Anya. "We expect there to be a Lady Lindley soon," his aunt had said. . . .

She was just about to slip off to sleep at last when she heard a strange electronic humming in the garden below. Sandy frowned, trying to identify the sound, but she had never heard anything like the faint, high-pitched staccato tone. Groping in the darkness for her robe and slippers, she went to the window seat.

A strange blue-white light was flashing in rhythm to the buzz she was hearing. It would disappear, then reappear as its beam struck a cloud. Sandy blinked. Like cutting whipped cream with a hot knife, the light bored a hole right through the cloud. The dark must be playing tricks on her sleepy eyes. She started to turn away. But then it swept the sky again and Sandy knew she had seen something—a high-powered strobe light for night photography? A laser beam for a *Son et Lumière* entertainment?

Whatever it was, at least one couple was being well entertained: Martin and Anya were standing in the formal garden below her window. Even from that distance she could sense the same intensity between them that she had observed on the plane. Martin's arm was around Anya's shoulders and they were intent on the light and sound show that was seemingly being staged for their private amusement.

Apparently being Lord Lindley was not only a lot of work but also a lot of fun. Anyway, Sandy was sick of being one of his playmates. Every time she renewed her brave determination about taking a small step toward friendship, she was struck by further evidence that, instead, she had taken a mighty leap into a love that could never end in anything but pain. Their worlds were too different. Not their economic or social worlds— she could handle the externals—but their real worlds—the spiritual realm of the heart and soul. And no matter how electric his kisses, she could never be one with a man, who, for all his refinement, was little more than a heathen.

So it was settled. She would leave in the morning. Make some excuse about wanting to get on with her sightseeing. After all, she only had a few weeks left and she hadn't been to Canterbury or to Stratford or to Stonehenge, or to . . . to. . . . For the life of her, she couldn't remember all the legendary places she had saved a lifetime to see.

## CHAPTER 10

"GOOD MORNING, MISS. Shall I just light the fire for you? Feels like a bit of a chill this morning." Barton was standing by her bed, a tray with a silver pot of steaming coffee in her hands.

Sandy pushed her hair out of her face and sat up, stuffing the pillows behind her back. A few sips of the hot liquid brought her eyes open. The fire crackled brightly, driving back the gray crowding in through the windows.

"Breakfast is in the dining room, Miss. It's buffet, so just go down whenever you're ready. Would you like me to draw you a bath?"

"No, thank you, Barton. I can manage just fine."

Enjoying the comfort of the fire and coffee in bed, it was hard for Sandy to recall the source of the weight she felt pressing down on her chest.

And then she remembered. She remembered everything: The rose garden alight with Martin's kiss . . . the sky above the formal garden alight with Martin and Anya's show . . . her decision that left room for no more light. She was leaving. She would pack after breakfast; no point in rushing off on an empty stomach. She wondered if there was a bus at the main road, or if one of the servants could drive her in to the train station at York without a by-your-leave from his lordship.

She entered the dining room as two guests, whose faces she recognized but names she didn't recall, exited, leaving her blissfully alone. No need to make conversation. As she explored the long row of dishes on the sideboard, and lifted each lid, scrambled eggs, bacon, ham, sausages, kedegree, kippers, and poached salmon were revealed to tempt morning appetites. The golden eggs and pale-pink salmon contrasted beautifully on her plate. As she approached the table a footman appeared from nowhere to help her with her chair and offer fresh toast and coffee. She ate quickly and was just finishing when she heard quick footsteps in the hall. Oh, bother, now she'd have to smile and make small talk.

But an enthusiastic embrace left no chance for small talk. "Sandy! How wonderful! I had no idea! Did my brother bring you here?" Karen released Sandy and rushed on in her musical voice, not giving Sandy a chance to answer.

"When did you come? I was afraid there'd be no one else my age here, but Aunt Miriam has other plans for a few days, so I must do my duty by the family. Are you having a good time?" And she turned to pile food from the buffet on her plate, hardly pausing for a reply.

Sandy's smile turned to laughter before her friend came to a stop. "Yes, yesterday, and yes. Whatever happened to British reserve?"

Karen plopped down in the nearest chair, giving the footman no chance to do his assigned duty. "I think it's the Yorkshire air. It's so invigorating. Have you plans for the day? You haven't seen Harrogate yet, have you? The flowers are marvelous. I usually go riding as soon as I get here, but the weather's nasty today." Karen was now emptying her plate as rapidly she had filled it. Sandy had another cup of coffee to keep her friend company. Maybe she wouldn't leave today after all.

"I wish we had a sunny day for your first view of Harrogate, but it's lovely in any weather," Karen said a few hours later, holding the wheel of her little green Austin with one hand and gesturing with the other. "This park is called The Stray. It used to be called the Two Hundred Acres. It was preserved as a public place when the Forest of Knaresborough was enclosed in the eighteenth century."

"It's lovely. It gives such a sense of spaciousness to the whole town."

"Mmm, just one of the glories of Harrogate. You should see it in the early spring when it's carpeted with crocuses—just as soon as the snows are gone from the moors."

Karen pulled her little car to a stop in the town square. "See that rather ornate gray stone building across the way? The Royal Baths. For about three hundred years, Harrogate was one of the most fashionable spas in Europe—said to cure everything from indigestion to epilepsy. They finally lost out in the 1920s when medical science outstripped them."

They entered an elegant turn-of-the-century building and were seated at a round table on small red tufted chairs. The waitress spread a lavish Victorian-style tea before them, complete with meringue swans. Karen picked up the graceful teapot decorated with clusters of delicate violets. "Royal Worcester," she remarked absently, examining the fine china in her hand.

Sandy laughed. "It sounds as lovely as the china itself when you say it. When I say it, it sounds like I'm lisping the name of a male chicken."

Their ensuing fits of giggles would have been improper for the young Victorian ladies that had populated the parlor a century before.

When she was able to stop laughing, Karen continued her cheerful conversation. "I tried to persuade big brother to escort us today. I think he was tempted, but the Hungarian Rhapsody was clinging like a limpet and couldn't be shaken loose."

Sandy swallowed the last bit of her meringue. "Hungarian? Oh, Anya? I didn't realize she was Hungarian."

"Oh, well, something Balkan—they're all down there together and always making trouble."

Sandy started to mention that Anya had come to England on the same plane from America as she. But she thought better of it. Changing the subject, Sandy requested, "Tell me about your family, Karen."

Karen put a big scoop of sugar in her tea and stirred vigorously for a second. "Daddy died when I was twelve and Mum has lived very much in retirement in her London flat and a country place in Kent ever since then. So in a sense Martin has practically raised me—through the difficult years, at least.

"He was pretty young then, too, to inherit the title and all. I guess you've seen how seriously he takes his responsibility."

Sandy nodded. The outline of facts was the same as Martin had given her, but she couldn't make up her mind about the "serious responsibility" part. Was she to believe Karen's testimony or her own eyes? Sometimes it seemed that nothing quite fit—like the old inn outside Winchester that had been built with only the carpenter's eye as a measure.

Karen, warming to her favorite topic, was oblivious to Sandy's lack of enthusiasm. "My brother's made of tough fiber. Everything he does, he does well—unbiased observer that I am—and when he decides to do something, he doesn't turn back, even when the going's hard."

She took a sip of tea. "Well, end of endorsement! But it does seem that trustworthiness and dependability are rather rare qualities today, and Martin's always been a rock in my life.

"That's what I first saw in Bill, too. Guess I was really lucky to find him. After all, a brother like mine is a pretty hard act to follow."

"Where's Bill now?" Sandy asked, again hoping to find a more suitable topic. She would hate for Karen to find out what a playboy her brother was.

"On holiday with his family. But he hopes to get up this weekend. I do hope so—I haven't seen him for just ages."

"When are you going to get married?"

Karen sighed. "Bill graduates next year. I hope we can hold out that long. That's the trouble with finding the right man when you're practically still in the nursery."

The pastry tray was depleted, but Karen poured another cup of tea for herself and Sandy.

Sandy added milk to hers and started to drink it, then decided she could not possibly hold even one more sip. "Are there any good dress shops here? The women all wore evening gowns last night, and I don't even own one."

"It doesn't really matter. I often wear street-length dresses to dinner—but this is perhaps a more high-toned crowd than usual—all that military brass and the diplomatic types. I suppose I shall have to dust off the formalwear, too. But don't worry, Sandy, you always look lovely."

It was Sandy's lucky day. The very first shop they tried had a wonderful dress—a peachy-pink fabric designed with long, full sleeves and a tightly fitted bodice, lace cuffs, lace yoke culminating in a high neckline, and a deep lace ruffle bordering the skirt.

"It's perfect!" Karen declared. "I'll lend you my cameo to wear with it. And you must have Barton do your hair up in a cluster of curls on top of your head. What a picture you'll make! The old generals will be quite taken!"

Unfortunately, the vision would have to be postponed until the shop could shorten the dress and deliver it to Lindley Hall. "Don't worry," said Karen, "it's worth waiting for."

When the girls returned from their expedition, it was time to dress for dinner. Sandy rang for Barton to press her primrose yellow dress, which had been mercilessly crushed in the hasty packing. Barton's ministrations were successful and Sandy appeared in the long drawing room, looking fresh and assuring herself she had her emotions securely in hand.

And that was true—until a mellow masculine voice just behind her said, "Here's the sunshine we've been missing all day. I think I was stood up in the rose garden this morning."

Sandy would have preferred to express surprise that he was up that early, considering his late-night rendezvous with Anya, but settled for a brief reference to Karen's spiriting her off to Harrogate. *Why can't I think when I'm around him?* All the attraction she felt for him welled up, and she fought to keep it out of her eyes and her voice, and began chatting lightly about the enchantments of Harrogate.

The effort was short-lived, however, for Anya appeared, wearing a slim, sleeveless white satin gown with a low neckline and skirt slit to the thigh, and quickly claimed Martin. He gave Sandy a brief nod and then turned all his attention to the woman clasping his arm.

Sandy felt hurt and lost at Martin's near snub. Fortunately at that moment she was introduced to a rather nervous, red-haired, ruddy-complexioned young man who seemed to be forcefully resisting the urge to tug at the high collar of his formal shirt. He did, however, offer his arm to escort Sandy in to dinner and she was glad to find that, though the seating arrangements had been changed, she was at Karen's end of the table with just the young man between them. Lady

Hugh was in Sandy's former place at Martin's left. But Anya, she noticed with a tug at her heart, remained at his right.

Sandy turned her attention to the young man. She learned that his name was James Harlan, that he worked in Whitehall, and that he ate noisily. His greatest virtue was that he seemed most content to have Karen and Sandy converse over his head. So dinner passed tolerably, with Sandy studiously ignoring the other end of the table.

Sandy was taking no chances tonight on invitations for moonlight strolls in the garden—Martin's excuse would probably be experiencing the formal garden by Braille or something, and she wanted none of it. Always schooled in honesty, her thoughts forced her to confess that really she wanted too much of it. But the outcome was the same. So as soon as Karen, in her emerald green chiffon gown, had led the ladies to the drawing room for coffee, Sandy made excuses to her hostess and escaped to her room.

She shut the heavy draperies over the windows, undressed, and pulled the bedding up around her ears determined to sleep . . . without dreams of distinguished lords in English manor houses. . . .

The next thing Sandy knew she was wakened by a knock at her door. "Yes?" she called sleepily and Karen bounded in, jodphur-clad and carrying a riding crop.

"Come on, slug-a-bed! The sun is shining and there's not a minute to lose. I've already ordered the horses."

Sandy rolled over and rubbed her eyes, "What are you babbling about?"

Karen strode to the windows and pulled back the drapes to let the morning sunlight flood the room. "I'm talking about *that*!" she proclaimed, waving her arm toward the radiant shafts streaming in the windows and lying in pools of gold on the floor. "It's called sunshine, and it's not to be taken for granted in a country where fish outnumber people about three hundred to one."

Barton arrived with coffee, which Sandy accepted gratefully. "Sunshine I understand, but what did you say about a horse?"

"I told you I always go riding as soon as I get here. You have no idea how glorious it is on the moors. Cook is packing us a lunch. We'll stow it in saddlebags and spend the whole gorgeous day out!" She threw her arms wide and spun around.

Sandy giggled. "I do hate to throw a damper on such exuberance, but I think you should know a couple of things. I've ridden exactly three times in my life, and I don't own a riding habit."

Now it was Karen's turn to giggle. "You sound like you're going to a convent. You have slacks, don't you? I'll loan you boots and a cap. You'll need those for comfort. And better bring a jacket, the breeze is pretty fresh on the moors." Karen crossed to the door. "Meet you at breakfast, but hurry!"

Following orders, Sandy hurried, scrambling into beige slacks and jacket with a high-necked white blouse that resembled a stock tie. She tied her hair back at the nape of her neck with a black ribbon and supposed that with proper boots and hat she would pass. "A man riding by on a horse would never notice," she grinned, thinking of one of Aunt Martha's favorite sayings.

"Well done," Karen approved when Sandy entered the breakfast room.

As the morning before, they were alone. "Where is everyone?" asked Sandy, making her choices from the sideboard's abundance. "You'd think we were alone on the estate."

Karen shrugged, "I don't know. Martin keeps them occupied, I guess. Some Home Office drill most likely. Suits me fine. I like being free from social obligations. Especially here. What with my dreary office job in London and all, I just don't get to the Hall often enough. Then when I come, I never want to leave—but it's better for the tourists if we aren't around too much."

"Tourists?"

"Oh, yes, the Hall is on the National Registry—open to the public weekends and Wednesdays. It takes pots of money to keep a pile like this going—even though most of the staff is only part-time—so all those six-shilling tickets help.

Of course, we don't *have* to leave when it's open, but one feels rather exposed." She took her last bite of sausage. "Race you to the stable."

The stables were off to the side of the house beyond the gardens. "You did order something gentle for me, didn't you?" Sandy asked as they crossed the cobbled courtyard toward the two horses being held by grooms.

"Oh, yes," Karen assured her, stroking the neck of a sleek bay, "This is Paladin. He's an old dear and has the gentlest gait."

"I know, like a rocking chair," Sandy laughed as the groom gave her a leg up. "Ooh! This is different! I'm used to a saddle horn to hang on to. I feel all bare up here!" She looked down at the sleek piece of brown leather between her and the horse.

"You'll love it when you get used to it," Karen assured her as she mounted her small white mare. "I sat a western saddle once in America and I felt so confined. We'll take it easy till you get the feel of things."

Sandy shot her friend a fearful look, but didn't reply. As they rode slowly along a path through the woods, the sun sifted through the boughs of the trees and made bright patterns on the soft woodland floor. Pools of sunshine spotlighted nestled clusters of bright yellow wildflowers—celandine poppies Karen called them.

From the top of a gentle hill outside the wood,

151

rolling green hills spread as far as the eye could see. Clusters of trees dotted hills and dales and long dark trails of leafy green showed the courses of numerous nurturing rivers. Tiny villages were tucked in the hollows between the hills and everywhere the smooth green was cut by stone fences, running in odd patterns like the lines of a jigsaw puzzle.

They sat for some time in silence. Finally Sandy sighed, "Yes, I can see why you love it. It's the sense of infinity."

They were almost halfway down the far side of the slope when the sound of galloping hoofbeats made the girls stop and turn in their saddles. A lone rider was cantering toward them. In a moment Martin was beside them. "Caught you sneaking off again, didn't I?"

Sandy was glad that Karen answered because she was breathless with the sight of Martin in riding clothes, sitting easily atop his spirited chestnut steed. "I'm giving myself the day off," he announced. "No sense being lord of the manor if you can't enjoy it once in a while. Where to, ladies?"

"If you really have the day off, how about Rievaulx?" asked Karen.

"Excellent!" he spurred his horse into the lead. When they were at the bottom of the hill he turned to Sandy, "Do you jump?"

"Jump?" Her blue eyes opened wide in alarm.

"I'm barely hanging on and we've done nothing but walk."

"You're exaggerating. You have a very good seat. I've noticed." Sandy knew he referred to her position in the saddle and not to her figure, but she still felt an impulse to blush. "Let's just try a nice easy canter. Don't freeze in the trot. That's the hardest of all until you learn to post."

Sandy nodded and nudged Paladin gently with her heels. "Let's see this famous rocking chair of yours, pal." She gripped the reins tightly with both hands, but controlled the instinct to pull back. After a few breathless moments she began to feel the easy rhythm of the horse's feet pounding the sod and her tension melted as she let her body move with him. The fresh breeze blew past her face and the sun beamed warm on her shoulders. The soft baaa's of a flock of black-faced Yorkshire sheep grazing on a hillside and the tinkle of a bell reached Sandy's ears.

Ahead of her Martin reined to a stop by a low stone wall. "Most of the walls have low places like this one where you can walk a horse across, but we'll stay close to the road so you won't get trapped."

Sandy nodded gratefully. They passed through the village of Scawton, made their way down a long, wooded valley that opened out past two farms and wound along the narrow little road over a humpbacked stone bridge crossing the river Rie, then turned and followed the road by the tumbling river until they rounded a thickly clustered clump of trees. There Karen and Martin stopped. Spellbound, Sandy beheld the sheer grace of the magnificent soaring arches of Rievaulx Abbey rising from the floor of the valley.

As with Ariel in "The Tempest," her mind flew backward through time and space to the monks who had toiled here for hundreds of years. When Martin dismounted and stretched out his hand to assist her, she shook her head to clear it of the images the scene had conjured. But Martin was real and warm and present, and the lean strength of his hands holding her waist as she slipped from the saddle brought her back to the present.

When her feet had touched the ground, he didn't release her, but turned her toward him and planted the briefest of kisses on her forehead. She pulled back sharply, her head bumping Paladin's warm neck.

"Why have you been avoiding me?" he asked.

Several yards below them Sandy could see Karen leading White Lady to the river for a drink. But she would soon be back. This was no time for a confrontation.

She shrugged, "I thought it was the other way around."

He scowled, "I thought I explained—I really have no choice. . . ."

"Yes, I know—emergency . . . or duty."

Still scowling, Martin watered the horses and then tied them to a nearby tree. He touched Sandy's elbow lightly and the three of them turned toward the Abbey.

They walked across the sheep-cropped grass flowing around the base of the arches and under the flying buttress soaring high overhead. The nave was almost entirely gone, but the choir and transepts stood to their full height, their rooflessness letting in the glorious summer air and sunshine, making the visitors feel at one with the nature surrounding them.

Karen wandered ahead and turned out of sight into the transept. Sandy and Martin stood side by side, not touching, not talking. Bees buzzed around clover in the grass; the stream below them murmured gently with its soft sound; the branches of the lacy trees overhead rustled and sang together. The listeners feasted on the fragile jubilee of harmony. Without really thinking about what she was doing, Sandy began to sing softly: "Were the whole realm of nature mine, That were a present far too small; Love so amazing, so divine, Demands my soul, my life, my all."

Then, all was still, as if the very stones were holding their breath, listening to her hymn. Only as the melody died on her lips did she realize she had sung aloud. Feeling a flush of embarrassment, she dropped her head, her downcast eyes moist.

"When I Survey the Wondrous Cross," Martin said softly.

Sandy turned to him, flabbergasted. "You know it?"

He smiled, "I'm not the heathen you think me to be, Sandra. I am a Christian, and I do attend church with some regularity."

Sandy caught her breath, unable to believe what she was hearing, "You *do?*"

He laughed gently at the incredulity in her voice. "Yes, I *do*. Did you think you'd fallen into the hands of an infidel?" Sandy blushed at the correctness of his guess. "Is that why you've kept me at such a distance?"

"Well, I've tried." She was looking at the ground, but the tiniest smile tickled the corners of her mouth.

"Yes, I can see that now," Martin looked at her with wide-eyed understanding. "I knew your faith meant a lot to you, but you had no way of knowing anything about me, did you? Maybe English reserve isn't always the best policy—but the more something means to us, the less we're inclined to talk about it. I think you need to hear me out." He paused and Sandy could sense that he was struggling to frame his thoughts.

"When I say the words of the Confession, I mean them," he began. "I do believe that 'He pardoneth and absolveth all them which truly repent and believe His holy gospel . . . that we may do those things which please Him, and that the rest of our life hereafter may be pure and holy; so that at the last we may come to His eternal joy, through Jesus Christ our Lord.' At least that's a pretty close quotation.'' He placed both hands on Sandy's shoulders, his brown eyes looking deep into her dark blue ones.

A breeze ruffled the leafy boughs outside the walls and a shaft of sunlight fell like a benediction on them. Their closeness in that moment was a glimpse of the glory Pam had written about in her letter—spiritual unity. Their hearts were one.

And Sandy's future opened before her with sudden clarity. This was the man she could share her life with. *All* her life—physical, intellectual, spiritual.

Sandy now realized how wrong she'd been— how narrow. It had simply never occurred to her that someone from a background so vastly different could share her faith. The wonder of it overwhelmed her. She closed her eyes and rested her forehead on Martin's chest.

When she looked up her face was radiant, ''Oh, Martin, I had no idea!'' and she stood on tiptoe to fling her arms around his neck. She clung to him, laughing and sobbing, while he kissed the tears from her cheeks.

And then his lips were on hers and she soared in the exultation that his caresses aroused in her, at last free to enjoy the physical delight of his kisses. Yet, it went beyond the physical; it was a celebration of oneness—oneness with each other, oneness with the serene beauty around them, oneness with God.

They turned and walked slowly from the choirloft, their arms around each other. "Perhaps I'm not as devout, as fully committed as you are. I can see a difference. But I'm willing to learn."

Sandy was speechless with joy. She had held a brief vision of one of the greatest joys life could offer—a life shared with the man she loved and with God. A preview of heaven.

"There you are. What on earth have you been doing? Come on, I'm starved!" Karen broke in on their solitude. As Martin withdrew his arm from Sandy's waist and they moved apart, Sandy felt as if part of her went with him, leaving her exposed and vulnerable.

They remounted their horses and rode across a half-mile stretch of lawn on the hillside above the valley. There on the wide grassy terrace, they spread the abundance of Cook's portable banquet. They feasted on thick wedges of ham and veal pie, boiled eggs, crisp dill pickles, chunks of tart Caerphilly cheese, small juicy greengage plums, and lemonade. And all the time, through the lacy green boughs of the trees, Sandy looked down, in awe, at the tremendous building below them and heard again the affirmation Martin had spoken.

She was so happy she could hardly eat. Her

lips kept smiling of their own accord and she wanted to laugh joyously at the slightest comment. Again and again their eyes met as Karen chattered on about the history of the abbey and the beauties of the day and the wonderful food. And each time Martin looked at her, Sandy felt the caress of his eyes.

Now that she dared to let herself really look at him with all her barriers down, she was amazed that she had been able to fight her feelings for so long. She looked at his striking features, his kind eyes, his slow smile as if for the first time.

Sandy's heart was so full in her throat that she choked on a bite of boiled egg and required several hasty gulps of lemonade to recover.

When they had all eaten their fill, Karen stretched full length on the sun-warmed grass. "Oooh, White Lady will never be able to carry me home now."

"That's all right," her brother teased. "We'll just take you to the top of the hill and give a push—you'll roll the rest of the way."

"That does it! You've gone too far!" She jumped to her feet and flung herself at him, but he was too quick for her and sprang out of reach. They raced off, Karen throwing handfuls of grass at her brother, Martin tickling her mercilessly. Sandy, packing the remains of their repast, was treated to a delightful scene of the very proper Lord Lindley and the gracious Lady Karen frolicking like children.

They came back, glowing and grass-covered. "Well, that's one way to work off our overindulgence," gasped Karen.

Evening shadows were beginning to lengthen as the riders returned to Lindley Hall. Martin helped Sandy lightly from her saddle. "Now, into a good hot tub with you. Tomorrow you'll discover muscles you never knew you had."

"Oh, dear. My legs already feel funny. I have to keep looking at the ground to be sure it's there."

"Steady," he said, offering his arm, which she gratefully accepted.

They walked along the path that led through the kitchen garden, its aromatic herb scents perfuming the air. A side door opened just before they reached it, and a voice with a throaty accent called out, "Ah, here is my errant squire! I have been desolate. How can I forgive you for abandoning me so heartlessly?"

And clasping his arm, Anya bore Martin off triumphantly, leaving Sandy to climb the stairs to her room on shaky limbs, and Karen to stare after them, dumfounded. But even though Sandy felt bereft by Martin's absence, she refused to allow that shadow to dim the day. Looking at Karen she shrugged her shoulders, grasped the handrail firmly, and took the stairs one at a time, like a toddler. Karen offered a sympathetic smile and closed the door to her bedroom.

## CHAPTER 11

INSIDE HER OWN ROOM Sandy gave a cry of delight. A large dressmaker's box tied with blue ribbons announced the delivery of her new gown.

After the prescribed hot bath, which restored her legs to full usefulness, Sandy rang for Barton. The maid's hairdressing expertise lived up to Karen's assurances and Sandy appeared soon afterward in the drawing room, wearing her blush-peach and lace dress and looking every inch a turn-of-the-century lady.

She caught glances of approval in the eyes of several of the guests and managed to blush prettily over Sir Hugh's hand-kissing ceremony. Martin, resplendent in his formal attire, smiled at her from across the room and then returned to his discussion with the distinguished gray-haired, mustachioed gentleman beside him.

But one guest did not accord her an approving look. Anya's dark eyes fairly snapped sparks at Sandy as the dark beauty rustled by in her cerise strapless gown. *An engineer's triumph, a voyeur's delight,* Sandy thought, her gaze following the daring cut of the dress.

Seating arrangements again were scrambled, and Sandy found herself between Martin's earlier partner in conversation and a man of striking military demeanor, wearing the dark blue uniform of the Royal Air Force. She was unable to decipher the numerous ribbons, medals, and orders adorning his chest, but was duly impressed when she was presented to General Smith-Barnhardt.

The dinner moved through its stately courses, and conversation flowed. Sandy was able to give polite, occasionally even witty, replies to remarks addressed to her without leaving her happy cloud of euphoria. Even the sight of Anya leaning seductively toward Martin could be viewed with amusement, not dimming the joy she carried with her from that afternoon.

Shortly after coffee Karen announced to her guests that they were all to move to the mirrored salon where a musical evening was to be presented. Sandy was most happy to accept Sir Hugh's offer of escort; the darling man and his refined wife were among her favorites at Lindley Hall.

The mirrored salon was indeed well-named. Three walls of the immense room were hung with tall mirrors in gold rococo frames. The fourth wall was composed almost entirely of windows, draped in heavy gold velvet, behind a row of Doric columns. The patterned golden oak and dark walnut parquet floor was set with delicate white and gold upholstered chairs beneath a sparkling chandelier. At the front of the room was a grand piano, a harp, and several gold music stands.

Martin served as a gracious master of ceremonies for the chamber music program. Sandy's favorite numbers were a Haydn string quartet, with each instrument taking the lead in turn, like a friendly conversation among equals, and a Mozart quintet for clarinet and strings, its delicacy of ornamentation, its intimacy and refinement perfectly designed for the splendid salon and gracious audience.

But Sandy's mind couldn't be contained in that room, as it kept carrying her back to Rievaulx, her heart singing with the Mozart strings. Martin was the man of her dreams: he wasn't hers, but at least she was free to dream, to release the restraints inside herself. Anya might put up barriers; Martin might put up barriers; but Sandy didn't have to put them up against her own will.

Incredible relief came from no longer believing that her love for God and her love for Martin were at odds—that she was being untrue to one in feeling the other. That magnificent trinity—

her love of God, her love of her heritage, her love of one man—could all be one.

The music soared and glided to an end and, as Martin rose to introduce the next number, their eyes met across the room before his duties claimed him again.

Sandy hoped for some time alone with Martin after the concert, but he was surrounded by his guests. So, bidding her escort good night, she ascended the sweeping stairway to her rooms. The harmonies of the music continued in her ears and Sandy knew she would spend a night of sweetest dreams. Nothing had happened to mar the perfection of the day—not even Anya.

And Sandy did drift off on a light, Mozart air, almost as soon as her head hit the pillow, a smile of contentment still on her lips.

The euphoria lasted exactly two hours and forty minutes, according to Sandy's bedside clock. She woke suddenly, unable to determine what had called her from her dreams. No strange noises outside her window, no creaking footstep in the hall, no wind wuthering around the house. All was calm and peacefully silent, as it should be, but Sandy was wide awake, her heart pounding.

She went to her window and pushed it open. The night air drifted in, fresh and sweet. A sliver of a silvery moon dimly lighted the garden below, and she could hear faint splashes from the fountain. The call to explore the garden by night was irresistible. Sandy quickly slipped on her navy blue slacks and pulled a dark burgundy sweater on over her white blouse, and tiptoed down the side stairway and out the back.

She breathed in deep lungfuls of the lovely air and walked slowly through the intricate maze of the formal garden, just visible in the pale moonlight. She was alone in this beautiful world. Alone, but not lonely, Sandy reveled in the tranquility, the peace, the privacy. She left the upper terrace and walked around the pool, enjoying the reflection of the stars, which shone even brighter tonight than the moon. A breeze ruffled the water and she hugged her sweater to her.

By the time she reached the third level of lawn, her eyes were accustomed to the dimness and she crossed the grass quickly. When she came to the gate in the hedgerow between the lawn and the woods, she paused. She supposed she shouldn't wander farther without a torch. Then she smiled—she must have become thoroughly Anglicized to think *torch* instead of *flashlight*. The dirt path that led between the trees was clearly visible for some distance ahead. Surely just a short walk would be all right, if she was very careful not to leave the path.

She walked for some time, protected by the leafy branches, occasionally glancing up to catch glimpses of stars overhead. Then a grassy meadow opened before her. Suppressing an urge to frolic on the grassy expanse like Bambi, she reminded herself that he had enjoyed such romps by daylight. Instead, she sat on a large boulder, listening to the quiet.

Suddenly and unaccountably the tranquil moment vanished, as if she had touched an electric wire. The unexplained disharmony, like the vibrations of a false note, was almost tangible. Sandy shivered and looked about, the disquieting feeling that she was not alone in the woods mounting. She held her breath, hearing nothing; yet the prickles remained at the back of her neck. She remembered the uneasy feeling she had experienced the afternoon of her arrival at Lindley Hall.

She had almost talked herself into relaxing when she heard the engine of a small plane in the distance. She looked up, unable to decide from which direction the sound was coming. Then the plane came into view to her left, flying low. She watched its blinking red light cross the sky above the clearing, wondering what its mission could be at this hour of the night.

And as she followed the progress of the plane, before her unbelieving eyes, a bolt of lightning streaked above the trees, followed closely by the sound of a clap of thunder. The whizzing streak of light struck the plane, spraying sparks like an arc welder's torch. The engine sputtered and died, and, trailing smoke, the plane disappeared behind the trees. A tearing, rasping sound of metal on wood and stone rent the night stillness as Sandy pictured the hull of the plane scraping branches from trees and bouncing over rocks beyond the woods.

Sandy sat riveted to the boulder, unable to believe that she was really awake, had actually seen a plane crash. As a wound hurts only after the first numbness has passed, so at that moment she felt nothing but a cold amazement. But in another moment she was on her feet, her mind racing faster than her body. She must do something, get help, rescue the pilot.

She started to cry out, but the scream died in her throat, muffled by an icy fear. And the same frozen dread stopped her feet. As she stood rooted in her tracks, her mind became coldly rational. The scene played before her eyes again and she realized that there was not a cloud in the sky. The lightning bolt had not come from the sky, but from the ground. Faintly from her memory she heard again the electronic hum from the "light and sound show" two nights ago. She had not consciously noted it above the sound of the plane, but it had been there. Something—or someone—was in the woods with her and it had purposely destroyed that plane.

Trembling now with fear and blind with panic, she turned and fled back toward the house. The path that seemed so clear only a short time earlier now almost disappeared in a haze of terror. She stumbled along, her brain as numb as her limbs. She didn't understand what she had seen, or what she feared, She just knew she had to get back to her room and lock her door against whatever was out there.

Wave after wave of apprehension beat upon her mind, breaking with bewildering force. Her body trembled uncontrollably, her heart beat high and fast, first choking her throat, then knocking against her ribs, then twisting her stomach.

Above her head the boughs of the trees closed out the stars and slim moon, her hair fell across her eyes, shrubs tore at her slacks. Something struck her heavily on the arm and she drew back with a cry of terror, only to realize that it was a tree branch.

Her plunge into the woods was purely instinctive, but she realized now that she was right. She must make straight for the house and Martin. She must tell him. Whatever had happened, there was a wounded—maybe dead—pilot out there. If she could just get to Martin, he could take care of it. He could handle everything. She longed for the sheltering comfort of his arms as she ran up the track toward the lawn, sobbing for breath, driven headlong by the nameless fright that gained momentum even as she fled.

Though gasping for breath, a stitch stabbing her side, sweat running under her sweater, her pace never slackened.

Suddenly a tree root across the path sent her sprawling. This time she made no attempt to stifle her cry as the painfully wrenched ankle sent shocks of pain up her leg. She sat for long minutes, rubbing her ankle and trying to think. It was impossible—she couldn't reason; she couldn't make sense of what she'd seen. But she could pray.

*Lord, help me. Give me a Scripture. I need something to hold onto.*

And the answer came as quickly and as surely as if the trees around her had spoken: "For God hath not given us the spirit of fear; but of power, and of love, and of a sound mind."

Her mind calmed and her breathing became normal. As she repeated over and over, "*not fear, but power, love, and a sound mind . . . not fear . . .*" The pain in her ankle was the result of her own groundless fear. Nothing was chasing her. She was in no danger. What she had seen had nothing to do with her. She had behaved like a hysterical child. She lectured herself thoroughly, resolutely refusing to give in to further alarms. She was alone in the woods in the middle of a dark night. Her ankle was burning with pain, and the rest of her body was shivering with chill in the damp night air. But her soul was still.

*Now Lord, please help me get back.* And gripping a nearby tree trunk for support, she pulled herself to her feet. For a moment she feared she might faint, but she held on, until finally, the intensity of the initial pain subsided to a persistent aching throb. Now she could stand. She groped around a bit on the floor of the woods and finally found a stick sturdy enough to provide some support. Hobbling painfully, she made her way slowly back to the lawn. She crossed the lowest terrace, then dropped to her hands and knees to crawl up the slope to the next level. The cold waters of the reflecting pool suggested a welcome relief. Pulling off her shoe and sock, she rolled up her pants leg and plunged her aching ankle into the icy water.

Her entire body shivered with the chill of the water and the air around her, but the numbing cold was the best remedy possible. The swelling and throbbing subsided and after a time she was able to make her way toward the house more quickly.

She locked the side door behind her and limped silently down the hall. How was she to go about finding Martin at this hour? She hated to waken anyone unnecessarily, but she must tell him quickly so something could be done for the pilot—unless it was already too late. She decided to try the first door she came to in the corridor in the hope that someone there would know what to do. She had climbed five stairs, leaning heavily on the banister, when she saw a light around the half-open library door. What wonderful luck! Maybe Martin was still up. . . .

She hurried toward it, then stopped and shrank

back at the sound of Anya's voice, "Wasn't it wonderful, darling! The light, she was perfect, no? The plane went *pouf!*"

Her throaty, triumphant laugh was joined by Martin's. "Yes, indeed, it was perfect. As you say—*pouf!*"

"And now your Sir Hugh and that odd young man from Whitehall can take care of all the boring details, and you, my darling, can take care of Anya."

In the light of the open room Martin and Anya paused, framed in the doorway, silhouetted against the light from the room. Anya turned and flung her arms around Martin's neck. "You have made me most happy!" she cried and kissed him.

Sandy saw no more, her face buried in her hands, but after a moment the doors of the library shut and they were gone. Sandy turned and stumbled blindly to her room. The pain came at her in rolling swells, tearing within her chest— a far worse pain than that in her ankle. She was in her room, but she didn't see it. She existed in a strange black limbo where agony besieged every nerve. There was a hammering in her head and she felt as if her heart would burst from her breast. Martin and Anya . . . Martin and Anya . . . what?

They had destroyed the plane and its pilot somehow with the light. They were together in some scheme . . . some plan that made Anya "most happy." As her mind replayed the scene in the study, Sandy surrendered to despair.

Of all the confusing emotions that warred around her, the most overwhelming of all was grief. A sense of loss—of bereavement for her vanished dreams. A world suddenly devoid of the Martin Graham she thought she had found loomed before her. Those precious moments at Rievaulx . . . she had really dared to hope. . . . But now her daydreams crumbled to dust, leaving only memories of beauty among the fallen stones of the abbey.

She was alone again—more dreadfully alone than ever before. She had glimpsed paradise, and it had been snatched from her. A wave of sickness swept through her as the thought that in just three weeks she would be back in her apartment—her empty apartment. The room would be the same; the view of the river the same; the unending stacks of ungraded papers the same. But she wouldn't be the same. Never again.

Eventually the tumult inside her began to subside. She became aware of her surroundings and realized she was still standing in the middle of the floor on her aching ankle. She limped across the sitting room, into the bedroom, and to her bed, but remained sitting rigidly upright on the edge, unable to relax enough to lie down. Now that she knew positively that Martin was involved with Anya in some way—had seen it with her own eyes and heard it with her own ears—she must decide what to do about it. But first she must force herself to believe what she knew to be true. And yet how *could* it be? Only a few hours ago Martin had spoken to her so compellingly of his faith. How could a man who believed as he professed behave like this?

And then she knew. He couldn't. Those glorious words of faith had been as empty as the ruined abbey in which they were uttered. For his own unfathomable, devious purposes, Martin was deceiving her. She had been right all along in her assessment of his character.

In spite of her fervent belief in the Scripture, she had to accept that the desires of her heart for Martin Graham were not part of God's plan for her life. And now that she knew, she must act. Like a sleepwalker she rose from her bed and moved stiffly to her dressing room.

She pulled cases from the closet and began filling them mechanically. She'd walk into York if she had to. Once she was on the train to London, she'd decide what to do next. A few swift movements made mayhem of Barton's careful unpacking.

Sandy snapped the lock on her last bag and flung herself onto the chaise to await daylight. When her activity stilled, her mind began to function. As when she sat still in the woods, the words of a hymn came to her:

Be still my soul, thy God doth undertake
To guide the future as He has the past.
Thy hope, thy confidence let nothing shake . . .
Let nothing shake . . . let nothing shake. . . .

And then she saw that she was behaving as foolishly as she had with her headlong flight in the woods and her actions would probably result in a similar disaster. She was behaving hysterically—not like a woman of faith who believed that God had a perfect plan for her life.

*All right, Lord. You're the King of my life and I know You guide my steps. I believe You have a purpose for everything—even this. Now help me find Your will in this situation. Be with me, please, so I can feel Your closeness and Your assurance.* She paused and struggled inwardly with what she knew should come next. *Yes, Lord Jesus, whatever Your will, even if it's to go on alone, I accept it. Just show me the way. Please show me the way . . .*

Her cheeks were streaked with tears, but the inner storm had stilled. Taut muscles relaxed. She breathed deeply, mentally drawing in peace and serenity. She could face it now—whatever lay ahead—with a still soul.

174

# CHAPTER 12

SANDY WOKE with a disturbing sense of disorientation. Why was she sleeping on the chaise? The sun was streaming in her windows. Why hadn't Barton brought her coffee?

A look at the packed bags on the bed brought her memory into sharp focus, answering the first question, but she had to wait until Barton answered the summons of the bell to find the answer to the second.

"I came earlier, Miss, but you were so sound asleep, I just hadn't the heart to wake you. Breakfast is over, so I've brought you a nice bit of toast and an egg with your coffee."

"Thank you, Barton, that's just what I need."

"Is there anything else, Miss?"

"Yes, would you draw me a bath while I eat

this? A hot one. And do you think you could find some epsom salts for the water?''

What with spending most of the day before in the saddle, turning her ankle in the woods last night, and sleeping on the chaise, every muscle in her body was screaming. Just crossing the room to ring the bell had been agony.

"Oh, and Barton, would you unpack my bags, please?''

"Of course, Miss.'' The perfectly trained servant—not a blink indicated anything was the least bit amiss.

Sandy smiled as she lowered herself gingerly into the steaming mineral bath. Maybe those early-day claims for the Harrogate Spa had had something to them after all. The bath and a few flexing and stretching exercises did their work and soon Sandy was glowing, reasonably limber and freshly dressed in her white skirt and pink blouse.

The deeper hurts, the gaping wounds inside, she stoically ignored. The day would bring what it would bring. She had committed it into all-powerful hands of Perfect Love, and she would await His answer.

Sandy walked to the window, leaned against the seat, and looked out at the beauty and symmetry of the lawn and woods with green rolling hills in the distance. Such peaceful green perfection . . . surely she had dreamed the whole thing last night. Nothing sinister could possibly have happened out there.

She turned and looked around the room, noting the grace and proportion of its design, the art treasures that filled it. She would never see it again when her visit was over. Yet, in a way, she would never leave it. Her soul had always cried out for beauty—a patch of pansies at Aunt Martha's; a small window box in her apartment—she needed beauty to relax her spirit. The beauty she had encountered in England, in Yorkshire, in Lindley Hall would always be a part of her. She would forever carry it in her soul.

She crossed the room and picked up the comb on the dressing table—a wonderful piece of antique boudoir furniture with a low mirror and a bench—and began brushing her hair. A knock at the door interrupted the rhythm of her motion. Supposing it was Barton again, Sandy called, "Come in," and turned back to her mirror.

Her brush froze in midair and she gave a cry of surprise at the reflection there. Not her maid, but Martin stood in the open doorway, his arms full of roses.

"I couldn't get you into the rose garden with me, so I brought the garden to you," he said. The room was filled with the exotic mixed fragrances Sandy had detected in the dark. But this time the scents brought with them a wave of nausea. It wasn't a bouquet she was seeing in his arms, it was Anya as he had held her last night. But what hurt most was not his involvement with Anya, but that he had lied to her about his faith.

"Sandra, you see before you the happiest of men. I've come for you to congratulate me. What shall we do to celebrate?" Even his words were similar to Anya's. Sandy rose from the dressing table and started toward him, searching for words that would not come.

But she didn't need words because Martin knew very well how he wanted to celebrate. He tossed the roses on the sofa and reached to embrace her. She pulled back beyond his reach and faced him squarely. Her voice was so quiet, so deathly calm she could barely hear herself. "Please leave me alone. I can't bear it. Just go away, please."

A look of uncomprehending pain filled his eyes and his mouth pulled into a tight, straight line. He turned on his heel and was across the room in three strides. The door clicked shut behind him.

Three minutes later Sandy was still standing where she had been. Her brain didn't even register the knock on her door before Karen breezed in.

"Hullo. What's the matter with Martin? I jut passed him in the hall and he was in such a brown funk he didn't even see me." She flung herself on the sofa, knocking most of the roses onto the floor, and threw her arms out luxuriously, "I've just seen the last of our honored guests off. I love it when we have the whole place to ourselves. What shall we do with our day?" Sandy still had not moved. Karen looked at her, puzzled. "I say, you look as bad as Martin. I have stumbled into something, haven't I? I'm most awfully sorry. Shall I come back later?" She rose to go.

"No, wait. That is . . . I don't know," Sandy spoke as if from a great distance. "Oh, Karen, I've behaved so stupidly. Martin came up to ask me to congratulate him and . . . and. . . ." She could force no more words past the lump in her throat. After a moment of struggle she continued, "I suppose you know he's engaged?" There! She'd said it. She knew she had to get it out and look at it if she were to go on living.

"What? I think you've all taken leave of your senses!" Karen cried as she stormed out the door.

With puppetlike movements Sandy crossed the room and sat on the window seat. The sun streaming in the glass warmed her. She closed her eyes. She could almost relax. . . . The door closed with a slam and Martin stood before her, "My sister informs me that I am engaged. I have every desire to claim that happy condition, but I fear the announcement is premature." He sat on the window seat and turned toward Sandy, but avoided touching her. "Now that we both seem to be a bit calmer, will you please explain to me what is going on?"

"I only wish I knew what was going on. But

179

the one part that seems perfectly clear is that I heard Anya say you had made her the happiest woman in the world—and now I'm supposed to congratulate you." She jumped to her feet and held out her hand. "That's fine, I do—congratulations, Lord Lindley. But if those kisses you insisted on plying me with were part of your English hospitality, you overdid it. You owe me and Anya an apology—whether or not you two have made things official yet." Her hurt had turned to anger and by the time she finished her speech, she was almost shouting.

Martin stood beside her and pulled her sharply around to face him, causing her to favor slightly her hurt ankle. "You quite mistake the matter. Things are entirely official between Anya and me. That is all they have ever been from the first—official *business*."

"You expect me to *believe* that? I saw you on the plane, remember? You were so engrossed in her presence you practically flattened me in the aisle. And as a matter of fact, you did flatten my suitcase in the gutter, you were so anxious to make her comfortable in a taxi. Official business, my eye!"

She shook off his painful grip on her arm and strode to the center of the room. "And I suppose all those surreptitious phone calls *and* your disappearing in the middle of the night in Cambridge *and* flying off up here at her beck and call were business, too?"

To Sandy's surprise, Martin sat back in the window seat, folded his arms, and relaxed his long legs in front of him, "And to think, I was afraid you didn't care. All right, anything more? Let's have it all—do you have me down for any more assignations with Anya?"

"Just one—two nights ago—all nice and cozy under my window, watching some strobe light show or something. And please don't deny you were with her—I saw it, remember?"

"Oh, no. I deny nothing. You're quite alarmingly accurate—have me logged on every occasion. And since, my dear, the whole thing is a matter of national security, and you obviously know far too much for your own good . . ." He drew his features into a sinister look, "I shall have to silence you in the best way I know how."

Sandy stared at him, amazed that he could be making a joke of this as he twirled an imaginary mustache, slowly rose to his feet, and came toward her menacingly. "You shall have to marry me, my proud beauty, then our fate will be sealed and you won't dare reveal me to my enemies."

"Martin!" She backed away from him. "This is not a laughing matter. Stop it!"

At that his mood changed. "Sandra, I'm not joking—I've never been more serious about anything in my life. I was just trying to get you to calm down so you'd listen to me. Are you ready now?"

For the space of a heartbeat she was held by his warm, level gaze. "I'm ready." She took a deep breath and sat quietly in the window seat.

Now that she was still, the atmosphere heightened between them and she could see how serious he was as he dropped his head in one hand for a moment before speaking. "First of all, Sandra, you must forgive me for bringing you into all this. I can see now it's been a terrible strain for you—even though I never dreamt you would see all that you apparently did. But I very selfishly wanted you with me. Dealing with Anya was the toughest assignment I've ever had and I felt I needed you—your quiet strength and your faith. I wanted to tell you all about it, but it was all so hush-hush I couldn't."

"And you can tell me now?"

"I certainly can. First of all, I made Anya happy not by proposing marriage to her—as a matter of fact, she's already married—but by concluding the arrangements of a very sticky deal for her political asylum—and her husband's. I had to smuggle her into the country, as you witnessed at the airport. She was supposed to be attending a cultural exchange in New York. Her husband stayed behind there to cover for her while we arranged the details here."

"Are they spies?"

Martin shook his head, "Not quite *that* cloak-and-dagger, just defectors."

"So all those emergencies that kept coming up. . . ."

He nodded, "Just when I'd think everything was running smoothly, I'd turn my back and there'd be a tangle in the red tape somewhere. I wasn't sure we'd be able to work through this last one." He paused, "As I told you, I work in the Home Office, something like your State Department. Usually I do routine diplomatic work, but this was rather more involved."

Sandy's impatience and curiosity were too much for her now that the crisis was past. "Martin! You said you could tell me—so *tell*! What about that airplane? I practically killed myself getting out of the woods when the thing exploded or whatever it was that happened."

"What were you doing in the woods?"

"Couldn't sleep. Went for a walk. *Tell me!*"

"Yes, my dear, but calmly. Anya's husband is a physicist. He developed a truly practical particle beam ray. But because they knew the Soviets would claim it as theirs by right, and the Gabrovos wanted money for it, Anya brought the plans to us. Our fellows set up a working prototype and then gathered here to see it tested before the bargain was finalized."

"I see . . . the general and everybody."

"Right."

"But wasn't the pilot hurt?"

"No pilot. What you saw was an RPV drone—remotely piloted vehicle, that is. We had to have absolute proof that Gabrovo's device worked before it was all final.''

Sandy shook her head, ''But isn't all that ray-gun stuff just science fiction—'Star Wars' and all?''

Martin laughed gently, his dancing brown eyes making her tingle all over. ''Not fiction at all. As a matter of fact, the high-energy particle beam ray has been somewhat past the experimental stage for quite a while. Gabrovo's innovation was in making the generator so small and relatively inexpensive to produce.''

''But why all this? Couldn't they just have defected?''

''Yes, but the Gabrovos wanted to do it in style. With a nice bank account. You've seen Anya—not exactly your everyday peasant commissar. She drives a very hard bargain.''

For the first time, Sandy giggled. ''No, she certainly isn't. A few more of her could set the next ten-year plan back twenty years. But why England? If they were already in the U. S.?''

''Highest bidder, my dear. That was one of the problems; they kept raising the price. It will mean most to England. Imagine what you saw deployed all the way around England's coastline as a defense against planes, bombs, missiles. . . .''

''Oh . . .'' Sandy remembered the day at Runnymede when she had quoted John of Gaunt. ''Now these beams can 'serve in the office of a wall or as a moat defensive to a house.' England really will be an island again."

"Right. We can never return to being the 'water-walled bulwark all secure and confident from foreign purposes' of King John's day, but it's as close as we can come in our world."

Sandy thought for a moment, searching her mind for the quotation she wanted, then smiled as she caught it: "This England never did, nor never shall, lie at the proud foot of a conqueror . . . and nought shall make us rue, if England to itself do rest but true." She put her hand to her throat, "I'm choking again. Oh, Martin, I'm so proud to have had a part in that! Well, I mean, I didn't really, but you—"

"Yes, my darling Sandra, you did have a part. Just by sticking it out on faith when you didn't know what was happening, you've been invaluable to me. As we say, you're a real brick."

She didn't feel like a brick. More like unset Jello. She glanced at her recently emptied suitcases and smiled back at him, then reached out a finger and touched the tiny crinkles by his brow, "I should have known that anyone with such kind eyes couldn't possibly be—"

"Be what?"

"A bounder," she finished, then looked away.

"Is that what you thought?"

"Well, you'll have to admit that your behavior was, at the least, rather erratic."

Martin laughed, caught the finger caressing the

side of his face and kissed it. "When what I really wanted was to be erotic."

"Martin!" She pulled back, but couldn't resist joining his laughter—so relaxed, so free.

"You can't imagine how I feel to have that weight off my shoulders. I've accepted lots of special assignments, but nothing like this before. I felt responsible to everyone from the Queen to the daily char who does my office."

Now it was Sandy's turn to strike a pose as she leaned back with her arms folded, "And now that you've been so brilliantly successful, all we've got to do is make sure the hush-hush stays hushed. How much am I bid to keep the lid on what I know?"

"The national exchequer is a bit thin at the moment. Would you accept one slightly worn Viscount from the Home Office as collateral?" And then before she could answer, he became serious and took both her hands. "Sandra, I do love you so very, very much. Will you marry me?"

"Yes, of course I will. I was so afraid you wouldn't ask me before my visa expired."

"Oh, you needn't have worried." He pulled her head to his shoulder. "We always carry on the family traditions."

And then, because the emotional strain of the past twenty-four hours had been so great, right in the middle of laughing together, the wonder of it all overwhelmed her and Sandy started crying.

"Oh Martin! Your beautiful shirt! I'm soaking it."

So he pulled her up on his lap where she could soak the other shoulder.

The sobs had quieted to alternate hiccups and little laughs and tiny soft kisses when the door flew open.

"You're wanted on the telephone, big brother. Some lady at Buck House wants to say 'thank you'."

## ABOUT THE AUTHOR

DONNA FLETCHER CROW shares many characteristics with her heroine, including a lifelong Anglophilism, a background of teaching English and drama in New England, and the fact that God has given her the desires of her heart: A husband as marvelous as Lord Lindley, four absolutely incredible children, and the opportunity to write cookbooks, children's books, and inspirational romances.

# A Letter To Our Readers

Dear Reader:

Pioneering is an exhilarating experience, filled with opportunities for exploring new frontiers. The Zondervan Corporation is proud to be the first major publisher to launch a series of inspirational romances designed to inspire and uplift as well as to provide wholesome entertainment. In order that we might better contribute to your reading enjoyment, we would appreciate your taking a few minutes to respond to the following questions and return to:

Anne Severance, Editor
The Zondervan Publishing House
1415 Lake Drive, S.E.
Grand Rapids, Michigan 49506

1. Did you enjoy reading THE DESIRES OF YOUR HEART?
   ☐ Very much. I would like to see more books by this author!
   ☐ Moderately
   ☐ I would have enjoyed it more if _____

2. Where did you purchase this book? _____

3. What influenced your decision to purchase this book?
   ☐ Cover              ☐ Back cover copy
   ☐ Title              ☐ Friends
   ☐ Publicity          ☐ Other _____

189

4. Please rate the following elements from 1 (poor) to 10 (superior).

☐ Heroine        ☐ Plot
☐ Hero          ☐ Inspirational theme
☐ Setting       ☐ Secondary characters

5. Which settings would you like to see in future Serenade/Serenata Books?

_____    _____

_____    _____

6. What are some inspirational themes you would like to see treated in future books?

_____    _____

_____    _____

7. Would you be interested in reading other Serenade/Serenata or Serenade/Saga Books?

☐ Very interested
☐ Moderately interested
☐ Not interested

8. Please indicate your age range:

☐ Under 18     ☐ 25–34     ☐ 46–55
☐ 18–24       ☐ 35–45     ☐ Over 55

9. Would you be interested in a Serenade book club? If so, please give us your name and address:

Name _____

Occupation _____

Address _____

City _____ State _____ Zip _____